INDIAN OCEAN DOCTORS

After three years on the beautiful Isles of Nowhere in
the Indian Ocean, Dr Helen French feels confident
that she can cope with almost anything. It takes the
disturbing presence of Geoff McLeod, the resident
dental officer, to make her realise that she is much
more experienced in her work than in emotional
entanglements . . .

INDIAN OCEAN DOCTORS

BY

JULIET SHORE

MILLS & BOON LIMITED
London · Sydney · Toronto

First published in Great Britain 1960
by Mills & Boon Limited, 15–16 Brook's Mews,
London W1 1DR
under the title 'Doctor to the Isles of Nowhere'
This edition 1983

Australian copyright 1983
Philippine copyright 1983

ISBN 0 263 74256 3

Set in 10 on 11 pt Linotron Times
03/0483
Photoset by Rowland Phototypesetting Ltd
Bury St Edmunds, Suffolk
Made and printed in Great Britain by
Richard Clay (The Chaucer Press) Ltd
Bungay, Suffolk

CHAPTER ONE

THE Isles of Nowhere, literally that is what Fan-Cho meant, Helen French pondered as the clusters of palm suddenly dotted the horizon, each cluster rising from its setting of brilliants as the sun caught the spray from the turbulence of waters breaking over half a dozen ringing coral reefs.

These were the Fan-Cho islands in the Indian Ocean, and she was their doctor, she told herself, trying to recapture the thrill of her first sight of them and the pride that title had given her three long years ago. Was it only three years—or had eternity stepped in and swallowed her up so that she now had no knowledge of time?

Funny how events had moved in threes for her. Three years ago she had accepted her first overseas appointment, and during the third month she had met Edward and fallen head over heels in love with him during the celebrations arising from his thirtieth birthday. It took another three months for him to realise how she felt, and then regularly he wrote to her, every three weeks when the mail-boat called at the islands. When he arrived on a supervisory visit her cup of joy ran over, for though Edward had never confessed his feelings for her in those letters, he had no compunction about making love to her in person. She was, after all, extremely attractive, if a little obvious, he decided, with her long, red-gold hair and serious grey eyes, and if his kisses assuaged the loneliness of her situation out here in the middle of the ocean, who was he to be a prig about it?

It was Charmian, the sister-in-charge of the mainland

base hospital, who had told him he had 'gone over big' with Dr French.

'Never took her eyes off you all evening, darling,' she had said with impertinent familiarity which he was too weak to discourage.

'I thought she was a sweet, quiet little thing,' he said, his vanity pleased, nevertheless. 'I'll write her a note wishing her well in Fan-Cho, etcetera.'

So had the correspondence begun and thrived. Edward Courtenay looked forward to Dr French's letters more than he would admit. Why, it had all the thrill of the unknown about it, for he had scarcely noticed the new member of his staff during his birthday party, yet here they were on Christian name terms and she was soon signing herself 'Yours, Helen', and then 'Your Helen', quite unequivocally.

Naturally he had been eager for his first supervisory trip out to the islands, and had been very careful not to include Charmian among his accompanying staff. He took two Indian nurses and an orderly, and thus he and Helen had been able to dine alone in her little palm-thatched house and really get to know one another.

She *was* in love with him, he very quickly realised. And he . . . ? Well—so much of Helen French was still unknown quantity that he was intrigued by her. She was a grand little doctor for one thing, and had studied her tropical medicine thoroughly. Perhaps too thoroughly. She was in the Fellowship class among physicians, but barely one degree removed from a schoolgirl emotionally.

He couldn't just drop her, he told himself, or she might break. He didn't want to drop her, neither did he want to commit himself. The women he had known were products of the sophisticated lives they led. He liked sophisticated women, found them amusing, and had long ago decided against marrying in haste, which made him doubly desirable to most of them. An unmarried male of thirty was a challenge to all the femininity in the unmarried females he knew, and the married ones invited him to their parties in order to revitalise their husbands who might be flagging in expressing those compliments which in the first instance had been the lure to the marital hook.

During the third year, however, Edward had grown to realise you cannot take love without caring a little. For one thing a fellow—an artist—had drifted out to Fan-Cho and actually set up house on Helen's island. They seemed to get on very well, and every mention of Howard Mitchell had made him more and more jealous of his sweet, virgin prize. He had gone out determined to ask Helen exactly where they stood. Instead it was Helen had asked him that identical question.

'Well—well of course, if you prefer *him*—'

'I don't prefer Howard. I don't understand you.'

'You know very well I want to marry you—'

'You do?' Her face had shone like the sun, or—what was it the islanders called her? Min Hana, white flower. Her face looked like a white flower awaiting the kiss of the honey-bee. 'Oh, Edward, Howard never meant anything to me. You don't have to mind *him*. He's so wrapped up in his work he never sees me—like that. Anyway,' she added proudly, 'I've never tried to make him. I once drained an abscess for him. I was at my loveliest to him at that moment.'

Edward was looking uncertain, worried. 'Look here, Helen, we're not rushing into anything, are we? I'm going on leave and then your contract's up. We'd better think about us. After all, it's a drastic step we're contemplating.'

'Drastic? What a way to think of it!'

'I should hate us to bust up, like so many do,' he fretted.

Helen looked grave, thoughtful.

'Perhaps we had better think more about it, as you say, Edward.'

'Well, it's for your sake, my precious. I can't help thinking I'm the only man you've ever really known—that is if you're speaking the truth about Mitchell—'

She had looked at him almost as though he was a stranger for a moment.

'Edward, you need never question my veracity on any subject. I haven't had the time or inclination to get to know men in the past, and after meeting you I didn't want to further my experience. I'm telling you the simple truth, but I'm not getting home to you. Either that or you aren't sure of yourself.'

'Rubbish!'

'Anyhow, go and enjoy your leave. If you find yourself not thinking about me, don't force yourself.'

'I shall probably think of you all the time and lose my appetite longing for you.'

'I should like to see you in that condition. Perhaps you'll propose to me again when you're "pale with love" for me, as the poet says?'

'With pleasure!'

Mocking a little, hiding her true feelings, Helen had let him—the beloved—go free, suspecting still, as she had done for some time, that occasionally things get a little one-sided, that there is one who loves and one who is content to be beloved, and that she, in this case, was so patently the lover.

'He would have fought Howard for me,' she pondered, watching the motor-cruiser, riding at anchor out beyond the breakers while the launch carried Edward away from her, 'like a dog over a bone. But when there was no question of competition he lost interest. Have I imagined it all? Was it really an obvious schoolgirl crush of which he was aware and yet too kind to let me down? But if that was so, he—he shouldn't have kissed me like he did; said those lover-like things; because now I don't feel like a schoolgirl any more. I feel like a bride left at the altar steps.'

Whatever Helen had felt then, however, was nothing to what she had endured later when weeks—which became dark aeons of time in her life—passed without a single word from Edward Courtenay. The visits from the mail-boat had no significance for her: a locum supervisor occasionally called on her with the sharp-witted Sister Kaye in tow, and she was complimented on the islanders' standard of health and reminded that her contract was running out.

Sand through the hour-glass: hope and time both running out together.

Eventually she was summoned to Madras, and the crowds and traffic soon put her head in a whirl.

In a whirl, too, were her thoughts as the Medical Committee tried to persuade her to sign for a further period as doctor to the Isles of Nowhere.

'A pity to let it slide, Dr French,' said the Chairman, an old, ex-army MO, 'but perhaps it's too lonely for a young woman, eh? After all, you might want to get married . . . ?'

'I never felt the loneliness,' Helen said promptly. 'I'd like to take some leave and think about it.'

Later there had been tea, and someone had mentioned Edward.

'He'll be bringing his bride out, then?' she heard a member of the committee ask.

'I really can't say if it's gone *that* far,' came the reply. 'I read of the engagement in *The Times*. Frankly I'm sorry for the poor gel. Courtenay's always struck me as being completely in love with himself.'

Helen hardly heard the voices around her after that. Edward engaged . . . ? Maybe married . . . ? It couldn't be true. He couldn't be so cruel and want to humiliate her so. He *knew* she loved him, and yet he hadn't acknowledged her existence in more than three months.

She excused herself and took a ride in a *gharri* round the perimeter of the city until she had assimilated the news and knew what she must do. Edward was coming back to India expecting to find that she had gone out of his life for ever, as a well-bred beast creeps away to suffer in silence. But Edward wouldn't be allowed to get away with it so easily. Having provided the hurt he must administer the healing, and the only cure for love is— unfortunately—to stop loving. Somehow she must learn to view Edward Courtenay dispassionately before she could feel free of him, and to do this she must be sufficiently near him to make the occasional meeting possible.

Early next day, before the molten sun could turn the streets into burning concrete, she went to see Dr Garland at his house. He was delighted to hear that if she could be granted three weeks' leave in the hills she would welcome a further short contract of eighteen months as doctor to the Fan-Cho Islands.

Without consulting the rest of the committee, the Chairman assured her they would be delighted to draw up an agreement on her terms, and he wished her well and arranged for her plane passage to Mysore. There were many Europeans at her hotel, and all the men vied for the attentions of the red-haired, grey-eyed girl who scarcely acknowledged their existence, and managed to look as remote at three feet as other women did at three thousand.

CHAPTER TWO

THOSE three weeks with time travelling at a snail's pace had seemed eternity to Helen, so that she imagined there must be as much change in all other physical things as in herself. The islanders would have grown older, there must have been births, marriages, maybe deaths of which she knew nothing. It was only when she forced herself to look in her diary that she knew the change was all in herself. She had received a damaging blow, staggered, almost fallen, steadied herself and could now afford to say, 'I'll be more careful next time, if there ever *is* a next time. No man will be able to say, what no doubt Edward has already said to his new love, that he was sorry for me because I was so obviously keen on him and that I clung like the ivy when he was only trying to be kind.'

Try as she would to forgive and forget, a little bitterness had entered into Helen French's heart, which felt like something from which the stone has not been removed. She was also a little ashamed at her hitherto obvious—almost blatant—femininity. As a doctor she now determined to play down the woman. She wore a severe white piqué suit and had screwed her pale hair into a tight little ball on the back of her head, so that her temples looked pulled and painful. She wore no make-up, not even lipstick, though her lips were red to the point of soreness as she had developed the habit of biting them with her sharp little teeth.

She was the only European aboard the mail-boat, and as such was treated as a VIP, for though the days of the

white raj were over in India, a doctor—and especially
one who worked for the government—was still someone
worthy of respect and due deference.

The ship was now slowing down and there was a jangle
of disturbance in the somnolence of the afternoon heat
as the anchor chain was released and rattled down the
peeling paintwork of the vessel into the water about half
a mile from the breakers ahead. The captain was now
bestirring his half-naked crew to man the launch and
lower it away. One or two passengers who were bound
for the Maldives or the distant Andaman Islands came
up on deck to see what was happening, but soon lost
interest. It was too hot for interest, for a ship in tropic
waters, without fans or air-conditioning below decks,
might do well to be called an oven and have done with it.

The two men manning the launch wore the *dhoti* of the
working-class Indian, and were true Madrassis, of an
almost aboriginal black. On the islands, however, the
natives were paler-skinned and orient-eyed and
favoured the pyjama suits of the East. It was difficult to
know just where, in this vast ocean, India ended and
China began, anthropologically speaking.

With Helen and her baggage into the launch went the
bundles of mail for the family of islands, for Fan-Cho
had five daughters, only one of which was too small to be
populated. There was a crate of cheap-jack stuff for
Simbat Lal, she noted. Simbat had unfortunately discovered there are easier ways of earning a living than by
tilling and fishing, one of the simplest being the selling of
rubbish to the poor mugs who were not yet wise to the
fact.

Helen shook her head and half smiled as she thought
of Simbat and others of her flock. Would they be glad
she was returning to them? They were expecting a new
doctor, though some of them—especially the children—

had wept when she had left them and begged her to come back.

Their parting song, translated, went thus:

'Min Hana, the white flower, is leaving us perhaps for ever. After the monsoon turns the islands green and water is stored in the wells we will feel no joy, but as though our sister was dead and we would mourn her. So, too, shall we die without her to care for us, for in Min Hana's hands the Great Ones have placed our stupid and ungracious lives.'

This decrying and demeaning of self was also a feature of the Orient, Helen realised, but she rather liked it. It made a pleasant change from some of the patients in the Greater London teaching hospital, who had thought themselves and their complaints so wonderful and unique and important above all else.

A rough awning had been erected over her, and with a final wave to the captain, she felt the launch suddenly reel away as though a small boy had tugged at a string. They chugged halfway round Fan-Cho and then she saw the gap in the reef, navigable only for a short period between tides. There were patches of exposed coral, the common red and the more spectacular filigree of the blue. The water, where it lay still long enough, was both purple and translucent green, like shot silk. The foam from the breakers made a ruffle of lace edging, and Helen wondered if the artist, Howard, had ever captured the effect as he sat in his little boat out here for hours at a time.

Howard would be gone now, she decided sadly, yet not sentimentally. He would have taken his notes and his sketching blocks and set sail for London and the Thames-side flat with its roof-garden, which he had described to her. He led a rather wonderful life which consisted of finding the few corners of the earth not yet tourist-ridden, living and sketching in them for a few months and then going home and writing a book about his experiences, suitably illustrated. These books made Howard out to be something between Robinson Crusoe and a Spanish Corsair, but they contained the magic of far away places, on which so many stay-at-homes were forced, by circumstances beyond their control, to exist, having neither the author's skill nor flair in otherwise indulging the urge to escape the daily round and the common task.

They were through the gap in the reef now and approaching the horseshoe-shaped beach. The sand one moment was white and undefiled in the sun, shiny as salt and lying beneath its shimmer of heat; the next, however, it was athrong with a dance of humanity, children first and then adults, craning to see, wanting to believe what they were told. The adults did an about turn and went to bring the aged from their litters in the bamboo houses, and there they all were, even Simbat Lal in the grubby drill suit he had taken to wearing, now that he was a business man, trying not to look foolishly pleased that besides his crate of new stock there was something else worth while in the launch.

How the children and the women shrieked!

'Shay Min Hana!' they shouted, pointing long milk-chocolate fingers. 'Min Hana cum!'

They all spoke pidgin English in addition to their own dialect, and often mixed the two, for so far the education authorities had not troubled these islands.

Helen was weary with waving long before a team of small boys rushed into the surf and tugged the launch up on to the shingle. Then, wet as they were, they claimed priority for the first handshakes.

It was just like being royalty, even down to the necklace of blossoms presented to her and the speeches of welcome from the headman, first of all, and then anybody else who cared to add anything, which was practically the whole community.

Finally Helen replied, for it was obviously the only way to get the beach clear again.

'Mr Chadrissie, Father of Fan-Cho, and all,' she said ceremonially, 'I am happy to return to a place where I am made so welcome, and my heart is very happy indeed at this moment. When I left you it was like leaving a part of myself behind, but now I am whole again and when I have rested for a night in my house I will be ready for morning surgery as usual. Will you excuse me now so that I can unpack?'

The headman bowed and smiled and turned away, denoting that the rest should do likewise. The women and little girls were loth to leave, and left their large, luminous eyes behind, as the saying goes. Soon there was only Simbat and two of his lackeys left, plus the boy who sorted the mail and sold an occasional stamp from his mildewing supply. Helen thought she would have to carry her luggage up to the house herself, then she saw her faithful bearer, Bahadur, approaching through the palms. He was a mute, but his eyes were sheer eloquence. He salaamed over and over again, approaching the last five yards on his knees and finishing up with his forehead against each of her feet in turn.

'Get up, Bahadur! That's enough!' she told him, touched, nevertheless. 'Go along with you and make tea. I'll come up slowly and cool off.'

So it was that when she entered the fan-cooled sitting-room of the small bungalow allotted to her, Bahadur had already set the beaten brass tray of tea and freshly sliced lemon next to her favourite bamboo reclining chair.

'Home at last!' she breathed, thankful for the privacy and the quiet after listening for three days to the monotonous beat of the mail-boat's engines. She surprised herself with that 'home', and yet she was subtly aware that Fan-Cho had become home to her after three years. It wasn't as though there was anybody in England worrying about her or what she might be doing. Her relations were merely 'halves' and 'quarters', as she had been the only child of only children. Her parents had died when Helen was still at school, and she had gone to live with Great-Aunt Maude, who was almost eighty herself, and seemed to make a personal effort not to pass from the scene until Helen was established in medical school, then she too faded away in her sleep and the young doctor was alone and rather frightened, afraid to depend on anyone or anything lest it be taken away.

But pain passed, and mental anguish—with time—became a sighing ache when it was remembered, and became harder to remember with each passing day. Perhaps it had been a wiser decision than she had at the time realised to return to Fan-Cho for a further term: if she behaved as though nothing had happened, full forgetfulness might well be the reward in time. So many women nurse their injuries. Helen was determined to cure hers before she left Fan-Cho again for the wider world outside.

CHAPTER THREE

'BAHADUR!' she called sharply.

She felt the servant's approach, for though he was mute he was not deaf with it, and so that he shouldn't be lonely and have nobody to converse with, she had painstakingly learned the sign language the people of his race used.

Refreshed, she was standing in front of a large canvas propped against the old-fashioned desk which was an item of official furniture and went with the appointment.

'Did Mitchell sahib bring this?' she asked, and watched the servant's fingers attentively for his reply.

Yes, Mitchell sahib had brought picture after her leaving. It was to be crated up and sent to memsahib wherever she might be. He, Bahadur, would have seen to it.

'Who—or what—is it? Do you know?' she then asked.

The bearer's eyes, black as coals, flashed in amazement.

Surely the memsahib could see it was a picture of Memsahib Doctoʀ? That was very clear. The odd thing about the picture was that Memsahib should have a tail—like a fish. There were hindu gods who had the heads of birds or beasts, but Memsahib Doctor was human lady with legs, as he—Bahadur—should know, for he not only saw them often enough but washed plenty, plenty stockings.

'Very well, Bahadur, I'll take your word for it that I look like any other white woman. You may go '

Helen looked again at the picture she had uncovered,

17

wondering why Howard—who had sketched her many times—should see her in this finished work as a mermaid, or sea-nymph, whatever the creature rising from the coral pool was meant to be. Fortunately for her own peace of mind she was a shy little mermaid, peeping modestly through the draperies of her long, shining hair. The pale flesh of the shoulders was bare, however, and there was a fourth-dimensional reality about the painting which made one think that when the reaching fingers found their grip, much more of the mermaid would be revealed than her hair could safely be expected to cloak.

'It's art,' Helen decided, 'and I shall have it hung up, over there, I don't suppose it would have been very flattering to be painted wearing my stethoscope. Howard apparently saw some semblance of romance in me still, though where it has got to I can't imagine!'

She sighed hard and covered the canvas from the dust.

'It would really have damned me in Edward's eyes, for he would have been convinced I had posed for the picture—like that. Rather a pity Howard's imagination went to work on me too late. I would have preferred Edward to have a reason . . .'

It is always dangerous to get lost in the maze of retrospective thought.

She unpacked what she needed, set out some of her books, saw that her bag was packed and ready for emergency, partook of a light evening meal and then dismissed Bahadur for the night.

The tropical dark had fallen more than an hour ago, and she had intended retiring early. Now she felt suddenly wakeful, however, and decided to sit out on the veranda to catch what there was of moving air blowing from the north-east. Somewhere in Outer Mongolia the clouds were forming which would be driven across a continent and an ocean to form the monsoon, distant yet by two or more months. Until then the night air was almost palpable with heat, for with Bahadur's departure the generator had been stopped and the fans were still.

Helen sat watching the fireflies starring the golden apple tree growing against the veranda, and in the reflection of a storm lantern hanging at a distance she saw pale moths investigating the paler petals of bauhinia flowers, which jealously secreted their heady perfume for the first touching fingers of the dawn.

Faintly, from the village, came the sound of rhythmic clapping and weird, tuneful chanting. Though she had tried to join in many times it was the rhythm which beat her, and her voice would soon be lone and alien so that she was silent and somewhat perplexed by it all.

It went on for an hour or so, and then—as though a conductor had brought down his baton—the chanting stopped abruptly.

The night felt empty now, and too quiet. There were no dangerous animals or reptiles on these islands, if one discounted the 'kossi', as he was locally called. The males of this bat family were occasionally known to play the vampire when there was a scarcity of natural juicy fruits, as now, before the monsoon. The islanders made life so miserable for the kossi, however, that he didn't often come near human habitations, preferring to turn in his desperation to the animal compounds and 'bleed' a pig or even suck a nursing goat.

Suddenly there was a sound Helen recognised as dry twigs crackling under a human foot. Because she was surprised her heart raced in fear.

'Who's there?' she demanded. 'Who is it?'

A human voice answered immediately, much to her relief.

'Sorry, please. I look for doctor.'

She didn't recognise the voice, however.

'Just a moment.'

She went along the veranda and returned with the hurricane lamp. Down below in the small area of cultivated garden stood a man. His upturned face looked jaundiced in the lamplight. She guessed he was a full-blooded Chinese.

'What do you want with me?' she asked quietly.

'Have letter. Please lead.'

The lisp charmed her rather and she smiled as she took the missive.

'I thought I knew everybody on Fan-Cho . . .' she said.

'Not know me, Mem. I be here two week only from Hong Kong. Call Ling John.'

Helen thought it was time she read the letter her unexpected visitor had brought. She slit the envelope and withdrew a single sheet of paper.

'Do come over for a drink,' she was urged. 'I doubt yours will be unpacked yet. My man finds his way by radar, but in any case I'll play my record-player at full blast.

'Cordial greetings,
'G. McLeod.'

'Well!' Helen scratched her brow. 'Does this mean I've got company on the island again? Fan-Cho must be getting known as a tourist's paradise or something! And what have we this time? Another painter? Or maybe it'll be a poet or a playwright. I rather fancy a poet myself.'

She had more good taste than to pump the servant, however. All she was required to do was to answer yea or nay to the odd invitation. Curiosity more than anything made her decide to accept. After all, one couldn't avoid anyone for long on Fan-Cho, and the sooner the preliminaries were dispensed with the better.

Fortunately she hadn't prepared herself for bed. She wore uncompromising blue denims and a biscuit-coloured shirt. Her hair was in a single long plait and lay over one shoulder. She decided against changing. After all, it wouldn't do to give the unknown Mr McLeod ideas. She was a doctor, and as such would perhaps take a couple of sherries with her host and then make her departure.

There was bound to be a heavy day on the morrow and she had known too many broken nights just recently.

As she followed the Chinese servant through a grove of bamboos she heard nostalgic, alien music filling the air like anaesthetic. Obviously Mr McLeod was no musician or he wouldn't murder Romeo and Juliet like that, using their tragic love as a gong to announce his imminence.

The newcomer had taken over Howard's house, as she suspected, and she half expected to see Howard lounging on the veranda, a veranda cluttered with half-finished canvases and sketching blocks and discarded paint containers.

The veranda was swept clear of all impedimenta, however, apart from a low coffee table and two lounging chairs. There was no sign of G. McLeod, though his presence was singularly intrusive. For one thing he was alternately singing and whistling the theme Tchaikovsky had written with a view to touching the human heart, and as he sang and whistled it happily, the indication was that he was heartless.

There was a pause in the general racket while Ling John contacted his master, then his voice shouted instead of singing.

'Shut that row off, Doc, and help yourself. I'll be out in a minute. Just having a dip.'

Helen lifted the needle from the disc in relief, then followed the servant out on to the veranda where he placed a tray containing a bottle of whisky, a syphon of soda and glasses on the low table.

'No, thanks,' Helen waved the man's offer of pouring a drink away. 'Have you sherry, or something like that?'

Ling John pondered this.

'No shelly,' he decided, rather than admit his ignorance.

Just then a wave of carbolic preceded the appearance of a very large young man wearing a very small striped towel round his midriff. The rest of his body was well muscled and brown from much contact with tropical sun. His black hair was roughened and appeared to be standing up on end. He had another towel in his hands and was busily drying out his ears, his eyes screwed up in the process.

'Sorry to keep you waiting, Doc, but I hope the Scotch is standing host for me. I'll just step into my pants . . .'

It was then the young man finally opened his eyes, scarcely believing what they saw.

'Good lord, a *mem*!' he exclaimed in sheer disbelief. 'You're a *mem*!' he accused.

Helen rose, feeling nettled.

'My name is French, *Helen* French,' she told him firmly, 'and I'm a doctor.'

'Good lord!' the young man repeated, in absolute dismay, and then—as the towel he wore began to slip a little—he suddenly realised it wouldn't look too good if the thing dropped clean off, in front of a *mem*, and bolted inside the bungalow to attire himself more fittingly.

'And what's wrong with being a *mem*?' Helen asked

the empty air, torn between stalking off in high dudgeon and waiting to have it out with Mr G. McLeod.

She decided on the latter course of action, and actually bolstered herself up with a whisky and soda to give her a bit of dutch courage for the inevitable fray she felt lay ahead.

CHAPTER FOUR

McLEOD's second appearance was a little more impressive than his first—from a sartorial point of view, at least. He wore a pair of slacks fresh from the press with a cream shirt and tie, possibly a school or college tie, though Helen didn't know one from another and was no wiser about her host on that account. The thick black hair was brushed flat, and the man was definitely good-looking in every sense of the word, though now there was a suspicion of hostility in his manner as he offered his hand and introduced himself formally.

The unfamiliar whisky had warmed Helen's heart a little, and she observed, 'No need to dress up for me, you know, Mr McLeod. It's too hot for ties and sleeves and—and things. Look at me.'

'I've already done so, thank you,' the creature said, pouring himself a whisky, 'but I prefer not to slack off myself. In out of the way places one either sticks to one's standards or grows sloppy. If one does the latter and slouches around in any old thing, it's ten to one regular bathing will be the next thing to go, and then—horror of horrors!—the toothbrush!'

The whisky had also removed Helen's natural shyness to some extent.

'Would you say *I* was sloppy, Mr McLeod?' she asked teasingly. 'Come on, now! Be truthful.'

He smiled grimly.

'I thought that was the last thing one should be in the company of ladies, Dr French,' he parried her.

Helen leant forward a little.

'*Am* I sloppy?' she repeated.

24

She stood up for his inspection, turned round and sat down again.

'Verdict?' she demanded.

He decided to let her have it.

'I was going to say no woman looks like a woman in trousers, but you do, and that makes you neither one thing nor the other. Yes, I think as a woman you *do* look sloppy.'

'Thank you.'

She held out her glass for another drink, waited until its warmth encompassed her and then decided to reply.

'Apart from the fact that I am attired most practically, Mr McLeod, it was my clothes which did not happen to be unpacked, *not* my supply of alcohol. If I had come here in something feminine and foolish I might have given the impression of wishing to stimulate your masculine interest, and that would have been wrong too, wouldn't it? I haven't decided whether I like you enough for that yet.'

Now the unfamiliar Scotch was talking with a vengeance! Without the stimulus of alcohol Helen would never have dreamed of putting such thoughts into words.

Geoff McLeod raised an invisible wall of steel immediately, however.

'Forewarned is forearmed, Dr French. Now I'll know your intentions towards me if you adorn that with which nature has obviously already endowed you.'

He bowed mockingly and Helen writhed. A back-handed compliment indeed!

Now she must always dress severely lest this handsome, arrogant creature think she was giving him a second thought.

'Obviously one doesn't assign oneself to Fan-Cho with a marriage licence in one's pocket, Mr McLeod; or can it be that *you* have sought refuge here from rampant females who find you irresistible?'

'At least there's more safety in numbers, Dr French. One rampant female could be quite a problem. A dozen I can handle.'

'I should like to see you so occupied. However, I hope it isn't too much of a blow to your ego that upon our initial acquaintance I—for one—find you quite intolerable?'

'Not at all.' He bowed and smiled. 'I'm distinctly relieved that the sentiment is mutual. Better to find out from the start, then we can do our work unhampered by thoughts of offering each other hospitality. Will you have *another* drink, Dr French?'

'No, thank you. I have a busy day ahead of me. Anyway, I'm not used to drinking with strangers.'

'Oh, come now, don't be coy!'

She stared at him.

'It happens to be true. Think what you like.' She rose to her feet and he immediately towered over her.

'Thanks for the permission, but I would in any case. It stands to reason that any young, pretty, unmarried female, virtually cast away on a tropical island, must have at least one deadly vice to indulge.'

Helen actually laughed out aloud.

'I should hate to disappoint you, Mr McLeod. What are you, a psychiatrist?'

'Nothing so impractical. I'm a dentist.'

'Splendid! I'm glad all that muscle is not going entirely to waste.'

His voice lowered half an octave.

'Are you playing a woman's game of trying to get me to kiss you, Dr French?'

'Of course not!' she said rather faintly. 'You've made it very clear that . . .' her voice died as the deep, blue eyes came to within two inches of her own.

'Then please refrain from making provocative comments. "All that muscle" as you put it, is attached to a perfectly normal man with natural masculine responses and reflexes. If you want to be kissed—if you *must* be kissed—I warn you that anything of such a nature between us would have a purely biological foundation on my part.'

'Ug—ug—er—' Helen said, weak with shock, and clutched his shirt to sustain herself. He obviously mistook this for an invitation, and she next felt her world blacked out as a pair of firm lips descended to her own in an experienced, confident, masculine demand.

She regained her drained breath urgently, but not before a second salute had been pressed upon her.

'Now, having paid the tribute you no doubt expected, I'll see you home,' announced Geoff McLeod clearly. 'Are you ready, Dr French?'

'Am I ready? *Am I ready?*' Helen asked angrily, not knowing where to begin. 'Just who *do* you think you are and what exactly do you think you're doing? No, I'm *not* ready to go home yet, and when I am I can take myself. As for your intolerably insulting behaviour, you can take that for a start!'

Her hand struck once, very hard, and she was no weakling.

Though he had not even flinched, one of his cheeks was now darkly scarlet.

'They all do that,' he taunted her, but this time she did not play up. She felt more like herself again, though weak in the limbs from one thing and another.

'You brute!' she said, almost under her breath, and walked slowly and unsteadily towards the veranda steps, where she stopped and looked back at her fellow European.

'You got away with more than you realise this evening, Mr McLeod,' she said quietly. 'I came at your invitation and did not expect to be assaulted. In case you need to be reminded, these are the Isles of Nowhere, not the waterfront at Hong Kong. Here one can still find the innocent and unsullied, but it depends what you're looking for, doesn't it?'

She plunged on trembling limbs into the darkness of the tropical night, still feeling shaken and dazed. No one had ever dared to kiss her like that before. No one!

Her anger was soon fanned up again into a blaze so that she walked without due care and attention. She tripped over a tree root and fell heavily. As she stood up she sensed another presence and her heart thundered wildly for a moment.

'Who's there?' she demanded.

'Ling John, Mem,' came the reply immediately. 'I keep small distance.'

'You can go away, Ling John. I don't need you.'

Of course, he *would* send his servant. She would have thought better of it if he had insisted on dogging her footsteps himself, despite her veto.

There was blood on her lip, she realised, as she neared her own house, and part of her upper gum was numb where a branch had struck her in the mouth as she fell. She went immediately to the bathroom and bathed her face in antiseptic, then used a couple of pieces of plaster.

'What a picture I look!' she told her reflection in her bedroom mirror. 'My cheek's swollen and I wouldn't be surprised if my eye didn't go black by tomorrow. I'm not sure where I hurt most, inwardly or outwardly.'

Once in bed under the mosquito net, she found herself wondering afresh, reviewing the evening's events and trying to be honest.

Did she really mind Geoff McLeod's kissing so much

as the fact that his kisses had been a revelation to her as a woman? Edward had not kissed with such assertive masculinity, and it wasn't as though McLeod had even been trying. He had thought she was slightly tipsy and would be easier to dispose of if he met her halfway. If he really cared about someone, one could imagine the mercury would rise until it exploded the glass.

Helen smiled—or rather grimaced—at her medical metaphor, and decided she had not come so badly out of the business as might have been the case. She was no more eager to continue the acquaintance with Tuan McLeod than he was with her; and it was possible to keep clear of one another even here on Fan-Cho.

If they met she must steel herself to behave as though nothing had happened, difficult as it might be.

What was a dentist doing here anyway? Dental health was perfect in her district. Native teeth were strong and white and clean, and only one old man in all the time she had been here had been entirely toothless. Though their arithmetic was suspect it was said that Ramtai-lal was one hundred and twenty-six years old.

From Ramtai, Helen grew to thinking of others, the beautiful children, the girls Mena Ho and Va-tu; she would probably see them all tomorrow and there was one case among her luggage which contained a small gift for everyone, meaning no offence to Simbat-lal, of course.

Her lip was now very painful and she could not ignore it. She reached a hand out under the net and grasped a bottle of codeines and a glass of water. A little later, as the drug soothed, she fell asleep and dreamt fitfully all night.

CHAPTER FIVE

THE swollen lip really troubled her next morning, and when Bahadur arrived with the early tea his fingers demanded to know the reason for her injury.

Helen decided against telling the bearer that she had been drinking whisky with a stranger and so had not been in full control of her limbs, for he was inclined to be narrow-minded about the activities of his memsahib. Even with Edward he had been wont to play gooseberry as long as possible, as though distrusting his own sex to behave themselves when alone with her.

'I fell last night after you'd gone,' she said with difficulty. 'I'm a nice one to see patients, am I not?'

The tea stung and then soothed. Helen's tongue began to play around inside her mouth, investigating. Finally a new horror beset her. She had knocked one of her teeth loose. It rocked alarmingly. If it came out she would have a gap, an ugly gap.

The thought haunted her through breakfast—she had asked Bahadur to make her some milky porridge—that having vowed to have nothing more to do with Mr Geoff McLeod, she now needed his professional services more than anyone on the islands.

But what an embarrassment to have to call him in to help after all that had happened!

Perhaps—she reasoned desperately—the tooth would 'fix' again as the gum healed around it, then there would be no need to tell anyone. But if this was a false hope, urgency was the password. Dental surgeons could do wonders these days if only they could get to work immediately a patient had damaged his teeth and gums. They were—as a race—all for saving teeth, no matter what they cost human beings in terms of agony.

Helen went down the compound to morning surgery only half-heartedly, wishing she had never heard of G. McLeod, Ling John *or* whisky, but everyone was so eager to tell her their news she actually forgot about her sore lip for a while, and was only reminded when the lovely young Va-tu, who was just thirteen, told her she was to be married to Simbat-lal's younger brother, and gave her a piece of sugar cane so that Min Hana could share her joy with her.

Min Hana unfortunately bit on her loose tooth and nearly took off through the surgery roof like a rocket.

'Is bad? Is not good?' Va-tu was asking in concern.

Helen controlled herself with an effort.

'It is very good, very happy news, Va-tu, and fine sugar cane. I hope you will both be very happy. When is the wedding?'

'Next moon, Min Hana. You come.'

Va-tu rose from her squatting position and sailed gracefully away. Helen's native orderly slipped a piece of paper before her on the table.

'Can you spare a moment?' she read, frowningly, and the signature read 'Geoffrey K. McLeod'.

Helen's frown deepened.

'Tell Mr McLeod I'm busy, Vikrit,' she said sharply, 'and that I'll see him after surgery if there's anything important to discuss.'

The orderly went off.

'That told him!' Helen thought with satisfaction. 'Why should he think I'd drop everything to see *him*?'

The thought of her damaged jaw made her feel a little uneasy, but she comforted herself in the knowledge that she had not dismissed the caller entirely, only until after surgery.

For the next hour Helen saw mothers and their babies, gave an inoculation and performed a vaccination. She then prescribed for a couple of old people and put plasters on a small boy's crop of warts. The last patient of the morning had a sore throat. Helen examined the man, suspecting the beginnings of malignancy. She told him she would like to send him to a mainland hospital.

'No!' he said, quickly becoming frightened. 'I not afraid to die. I afraid of sea. My grandfather he eat up by serpent.'

'Nonsense!' said Helen sharply. 'There aren't such things. If you go to hospital there's no reason why you should die, and when you come back you'll be a travelled man and be able to tell many stories of the wonderful places you've seen.'

The patient left, still dubious, but Helen knew the seed of healing was sown. The man was curious as to what did lie beyond these islands and would never have the means of knowing in the normal course of events, but it was too big a venture to assimilate in a matter of moments. Later, when he had thought about things, he would be back, enquiring about the next step now that the advice had been given. No man in his right mind deliberately chooses death if there is any way out of it, as Helen knew from experience.

A sensation of expectancy, now that she was free, surged in her breast.

'Where is he, Vikrit?' she asked, and, as the orderly stared, 'Mr McLeod. I said I'd see him after surgery.'

'Oh, *that* man,' said the orderly, with a shrug. 'I had forgot. He does not stay, memsahib doctor. I tell him your message and he smile, say ta-ta and go!'

'"Say ta-ta and go!"' Helen grumbled under her breath.

'I suppose he thought I should have seen him there and then,' she said aloud. 'Some people have no consideration for others and their affairs.'

'He said not important,' Vikrit shrugged again, turning off the kerosene steriliser and reaching in to bring out the shining instruments. '*You* say *if* important, memsahib doctor, and he say *not* important, only somet'ing or odder.'

Occasionally Vikrit rattled Helen to the point where she could cheerfully have struck him. He had had a very limited hospital training to fit him for his job and thought himself a very fine fellow indeed.

'What wasn't important?' she now demanded. 'Did he say?'

'It was—I t'ink—memsahib's health he ask. Yes, he say not important, only to ask how you are today. I say fine, an' he—'

Helen's frown told the orderly something was decidedly amiss.

'Do I look fine?' she demanded.

Vikrit at last realised he was on the carpet and decided to watch out for himself.

'I sorry if offend,' he said with practised humility. 'Memsahib doctor say "Tell that man I busy". It was not Vikrit who say this but speak your words. "If important," you say, and "not important" that man say.'

'All right,' Helen said with some asperity. 'It wasn't your fault. Perhaps you'll take a note to Mr McLeod for me?'

Vikrit agreed and Helen drew a sheet of paper towards her, biting hard on her pen as she did so.

Keep it in the third person, she grimly decided, and then wrote:

'Dr French regrets having missed Mr McLeod when he called and would appreciate an early appointment to see him.'

With this impersonal missive Vikrit departed for the interior of the island, and Helen locked up the surgery and walked slowly back to the house.

It was unbearably hot by midday. No doubt it was pretty warm in Hong Kong too, at times, but she was fairly certain that the nucleus of all the heat still exuded by volcanic earth was somewhere in this molten ocean, and that Fan-Cho was not far away from it.

Bahadur was awaiting her, chiding on his fingers that she was neither wearing a hat nor carrying an umbrella.

He meant umbrella too, not parasol. The bigger and blacker the umbrella the deeper the shade, which at least gave an illusion of coolness.

'Don't bully me,' pleaded Helen wearily. 'I've got toothache. Vikrit will be coming with a message from the new dentist.'

'Piece of string best, quickest,' Bahadur's fingers told her, then he offered his services.

'No, thanks.'

Helen thankfully sank up to her neck in the tepid water of the waiting bath. She heard Bahadur collect her clothes from the other side of the screen. When her linen was washed and hanging out to dry the servant would go and take his siesta until four-thirty, or thereabouts.

She stepped out of the bath and into the folds of a bleached towelling robe. Her toothache was really quite maddening and it was time Vikrit was back with a reply to her note. Surely he wouldn't have the audacity to clear off for his afternoon's sleep without giving her a message?

Audacious—or cunning—he had been to some extent, for she found a sealed envelope addressed to her lying on the desk.

Obviously the messenger had returned while she was in the bath and sneaked off before he could be asked to go more errands.

Helen slit the envelope and read:

'Mr McLeod thanks Dr French for her letter and questions the wisdom of making *appointments* in view of a mutually acknowledged lack of sympathy.'

'Oh!' Helen smote the desk hard in her exasperation. 'He's taken the whole thing *personally*! I wish I could hit him again, only harder. Oh, my tooth!'

She hugged her cheek miserably, knowing it was no use to lie down in bed with her nerves jangling.

'I think I'm a man-hater,' she wailed, drawing a sheet of paper towards her once again.

'Last night was last night,' she wrote baldly. 'Can't you see that this time I really *need* you?'

She didn't sign the letter, not considering it necessary. She then went to Bahadur's quarters and roused him as from the grave. He looked at her through black, sleep-veiled eyes.

'Sorry, Bahadur! I want you to take this letter to the dentist. He lives in Mitchell Sahib's house.'

The Pathan rose and scratched himself all over.

'I'll go myself if you like,' Helen said.

Bahadur said he did not like, and Memsahib was not to say such things. Was he Memsahib's bearer or was Memsahib *his* servant? If one was born to be a bearer one did as one was told, sleep-time or not.

When he had wound his turban about his black, plastered hair he set off into the shade of the forest, and once more Helen prepared to wait for the relief which hourly was growing more necessary to her very existence. To think that only this morning she had had the creature within her grasp and had let him go! A sop to her pride at the time, her airy gesture now was being paid for in full. She was past being proud now, and almost ran to meet Bahadur when she saw him coming back through the trees, the sweat running down his broad, brown chest.

Eagerly she snatched the soiled envelope from his hands and tore it open.

'Mr McLeod is puzzled by the tone of the letter he has just received (unsigned). If Dr French *needs* the writer after such short acquaintance, said writer is catching the next boat back to the Far East and is going into hiding meanwhile!'

'He can't mean it!' Helen said in sheer desperation. 'He can't be such a confirmed egotist as to think I need him in any but a professional capacity?'

Bahadur was staring at her in concern. Memsahib was going to cry: he knew the signs. Once before he had seen her cry and it had hurt him where his heart was.

'What is the matter?' his hands fluttered at her. 'I pull tooth with string. Very good. No pain at all.'

'No!' she shouted. 'Oh, Bahadur, stop bothering me!'

He followed her into the house again, however, his hands still fluttering.

'Is it man? Dentist man? That man laughs when he writes letter for Memsahib . . .'

'Oh, does he?' Helen asked grimly.

'He also say something, besides the writing.'

'Well?' Helen asked sharply. 'What had Mr Clever McLeod to say?'

'He say you want, you know where to find, Memsahib. After five-thirty.'

It was with mixed feelings of relief and absolute fury that Helen took more codeine and lay down at last on her bed to relax, if not to sleep.

CHAPTER SIX

LITTLE did Helen French know about her own self, apparently, she concluded, as she sat, simmering, in a small room next to what Geoff McLeod called his 'theatre'.

If asked to describe herself to a stranger she would probably have said. 'Oh, I'm just ordinary, I suppose. I'm fairly easy-going and prefer to be unobtrusive. I'm easily hurt myself and so try not to—hurt other people.'

'This *was* Helen French', might now have been her epitaph. A new Helen had been born almost overnight, a woman who now sat planning the worst she could imagine happening to a young man who had crossed her path like a meteor and determinedly—no matter how innocently—caused this metamorphosis in her.

A series of explosions were taking place in Helen's brain, and each one caused her to see redder than before.

How dare the fellow kiss her as—as though she was a casual pick-up!

How dared he break in in the middle of her morning surgery and expect her to drop everything and run to him!

How dared he make light of her urgent requests to receive his professional attentions!

How dared he 'tut-tut' over the state of her poor sore mouth and then proceed to lay her trouble at the door of her 'drinking bouts'!

Finally, how dared he fill her mouth with local anaesthetic and then send her in here to 'freeze' while he cheerfully carried on seeing other patients as though she had ceased to exist!

She had been 'freezing' for almost an hour, and in the next room she could hear the now hateful voice dictating to his secretary, a Chinese girl, who had not exactly been overjoyed to see Helen, though her expression was 'deadpan', the sloe eyes merely regarding the newcomer with insolent persistence.

Helen could stand being ignored no longer. She tapped on the theatre door and opened it, only to feel immediately ridiculous because her tongue had frozen too, and was cleaving to the roof of her mouth.

'Yes . . . ?' the dental surgeon asked offhandedly, then became offensively patient. 'Just one moment, Dr French, if you don't mind. I hadn't forgotten you. When I've finished this report we'll continue, but Miss Huong is already doing overtime.'

'I don't mind, sir,' the girl said in perfect English.

'I know that, Wild Blossom,' he told her teasingly, 'but *I* mind. You have your studies, and our sojourn here is an ideal opportunity for you to catch up. Now, where were we?'

Helen went back to her waiting, slamming the door behind her just a little.

'*Am* I being unfair?' she asked herself, and tried to simmer down a little. 'It's reasonable that he clears the way if I'm to be a long job. It's just that I never disliked anyone so intensely before, I suppose, and that being so he can do nothing right in my eyes. Once I get my tooth fixed I must resolve to keep my distance from him. I won't let him make me so angry, because obviously it amuses him to see me enraged, and I'm certainly not on Fan-Cho for *his* entertainment.'

She felt calmer when at last she was summoned back to the theatre.

Miss Huong had left, and Ling John floated about in the background in an unfamiliar green gown, obviously roped in to assist if necessary.

'You can't talk, can you?' the dentist asked casually. 'That's just as well because I hate being interrupted. This is a nasty mess you've made of yourself, and as a doctor you surprise me. Physician heal thyself with a vengeance! If you couldn't slap penicillin into yourself, why didn't you come to me earlier?'

Helen made a few inarticulate noises, but her head was thrust back unceremoniously against the leather rest of the tip-back chair.

'Shut up, do, Dr French, or you'll be sick. If you're trying to say that somewhat tedious correspondence you indulged in was because of *this*, then you might have mentioned the actual trouble instead of beating about the bush so much.'

He paused in the swabbing of her gum to smile maliciously into her blazing eyes; eyes which had been, at one time, likened to 'grey April rain-pools at twilight'. Now they flashed twin daggers at him until he inadvertently found an exposed nerve and they became blanks of bewilderment before filling with unexpected tears.

'This *is* going to hurt, you know,' Geoff McLeod now explained, more gently. 'The whole area's sore. I can't move without jabbing something bruised or swollen or raw.'

He suspended operations.

'Would you like us to leave it for now?'

Helen shook her head vigorously.

'I thought not. For my part I don't want you to lose that tooth. You've got a fine set, Dr French, and when you're feeling happier I want you to give me details of your diet, your eating habits as a child and so forth. That's why I'm here, you know. Not as a dental operator but as a scientist. The people in these remote island groups have the best teeth in the world. They don't clean 'em, they don't put them in a jar every night, they just *use* 'em. My work is to find out what they eat, what minerals are in the water they drink, etcetera. They're an inquisitive lot, aren't they? I asked for volunteers when I arrive—and blow me if the entire population didn't turn up to see me, even the oldest inhabitant!'

Helen relaxed ever so slightly as the probe, which had accompanied the soliloquy, now became reasonably bearable in its investigation.

'Perhaps it's not as bad as I thought,' the voice went on, impersonally. 'The secondaries made things look a lot worse. I'm going to use wire and make the adjoining, firm teeth responsible for their sick companion. You must eat on the other side only for a while. I think you'll find it'll settle down in a week or two, especially if you keep yourself fit.'

The local anaesthetic was now beginning to wear off, and Helen was miserably conscious of everything that was going on, the agonising tightening of the gold wire as it pulled the recalcitrant tooth into place and then the ramming home of various plugs and wire pins.

'There! You can relax now, Dr French.'

Opening her eyes, she realised that her hands were clutching the chair arms to such an extent that they looked white and bloodless.

'Oh. Is it over?' she asked thickly.

'Yes. And you've been very brave. I know it hurt like hell. People sometimes think we take a fiendish delight in tormenting them, but it's not so. Unlike you doctors, we can't always put our patients completely to sleep, especially if we need their co-operation.'

'That's all right, Mr McLeod. I *do* understand,' she

assured him, her limbs feeling light and trembly after the intensity of their contraction.

'Here. Drink this to steady you.'

He thrust a small glass into her hands.

She had merely sniffed and discovered it was whisky when she looked up at him questioningly. He was regarding her somewhat anxiously.

'One's all right, that size,' he explained, 'but I shouldn't go in for it much until you're eating adequately again.'

For a moment she didn't know what to think, then the humour of the situation was too much for her. She started to laugh, weakly at first, then with a real abandon that had him wondering.

'You really think I'm an alcoholic, don't you?' she chortled. 'I never heard anything so—so funny in all my life!'

She put the whisky-tot down on the glass-topped table.

'Don't you want it?' he asked blankly.

'No, thanks.' She laughed again, then controlled herself with an effort. 'I think I'll go home and—and open a bottle.'

Now *he* was at a disadvantage. He didn't know whether she was serious or not.

'I'll take you home, Dr French,' he almost snapped. 'At least I'll make sure you get that far without incident.'

'No need to disturb yourself,' she said blandly. 'I've seen my man looking in at the window for some time now. You're not the only one who feels anxious about me, you know.'

Another breathless little giggle escaped her, then she straightened her face with an effort, trying to compose herself to give the formal expressions of thanks and gratitude.

He dismissed these, however, somewhat impatiently.

'You were a job, Dr French. Just a job. I'd better see you on Thursday, the same time.'

'I'm sorry, Mr McLeod, I'll be on one of the other islands on Thursday.'

'That's too bad,' he said, putting his implements away. 'A pity to lose the tooth for a—a ha'porth of enamel.'

'Couldn't you make it Friday?'

He turned and regarded her almost pityingly.

'I'm sorry, Doctor, but I'll be away on one of the other islands on Friday.'

For a full minute she looked into the clear blue eyes of the man she felt she loathed, then she lowered her own and turned away.

'Very well. I'll try to make it on Thursday. Goodnight, Mr McLeod.'

She almost fell over Bahadur in her haste and irritation, and her thoughts were peculiarly unkind.

'One day, before he leaves Fan-Cho, that man may become ill and need *me*. Then it will be *my* turn to have him at my mercy for a while. I can hardly wait for that moment!'

Some of the houses crept down almost to the silver-sanded beach, and they were temporary structures of palm and bamboo tied together with ropes of creeper stems. Each house contained a living-room and a sleeping apartment, and there was a doorway over which was draped a brilliant length of carpet, the patterns being to a Fan-Cho family what a coat of arms is to British aristocracy.

Helen was visiting one of the smaller islands, which—though having no official name—was known to its inhabitants as Ay-oh.

Here on Ay-oh were five families only, soon to be increased to six, for the girl Va-tu was to live here after her marriage. Her husband-to-be was even now building a new house, watched and criticised by all the unoccupied members of the island community, chiefly the young children.

Helen was greeted joyously, and proceeded to hand out small bags of sweets to the tots, then she approached the nearest house and called out.

'Min Hana!' a woman shrieked, and Helen was admitted to the dark interior, blinking her eyes until they became accustomed to the half light.

The scene was one she well knew. In the centre of the room was the family loom upon which hung a half-finished carpet. The predominant colours of the design were a clear red and a violet blue with a thin outlining of white here and there.

An old man and a thin wiry boy were weaving industriously, and a beautiful girl-child of about twelve was working a foot-treadle which did wonderful things in feeding the yarn through. The woman who had greeted Helen so gladly had been carding the rough mohair and wool from the island's sheep and goats when she had been distracted. Now all the family paused to have a gossip.

'Where is your mother, M'ala?' Helen asked the woman. 'I hope she is well?'

'She is well, Min Hana. She is old and sleeps much. Come, I will show you.'

Helen followed her into the bedroom and knelt down beside the old woman, automatically seeking the knotted wrist for the pulse.

The old woman awoke and looked up blankly, as one who nowadays spent most of her time in another world.

'The old one—she says foolish things,' the daughter confided, yet without impatience, for family unity and love was the mainstay of these islands.

'Min Hana!' quavered the old woman, and then proceeded to examine, wonderingly, the whiteness of the hands so near her own. She rambled off into a dialect Helen didn't understand, and the woman M'ala began to giggle.

'Now the foolishness is starting,' she said, girlishly holding her quivering lips with a chiding finger. 'The old one says you should marry and have children as white as lily-petals of your own, Min-Hana. She says there is already one you love—'

'Quite wrong!' Helen contradicted blithely, 'but I like having my fortune told. What else does she say?'

M'ala looked puzzled.

'Such foolishness! It doesn't make sense. That hate so easily changes to love, but that a moth can never change into a butterfly. That is enough nonsense for one day, isn't it?'

Helen pondered love and hate and moths and butterflies until her head buzzed, while Vikrit steered the motorboat safely through the coral and into the bay beyond. Fortunately she had found her outer island families in the best of health and so had been able to return to the main island in time for her evening appointment with Geoff McLeod.

Now there was a man she loathed—and it was hardly likely such an emotion would turn to love. She couldn't conceive loving a man who so obviously liked himself well enough for two.

As for moths and butterflies—well they simply weren't relevant. She supposed, if one thought in such terms, that Edward was a moth and McLeod a big, flamboyant butterfly.

It was foolishness, though, to take an old woman's predictions seriously, or even give them a second thought.

CHAPTER SEVEN

ONCE her damaged mouth was healed and the suspect tooth pronounced firm as a rock once more, it was not difficult to have nothing to do with Geoff McLeod.

He seemed equally intent upon leaving her to her own part of the island, and rarely—if ever—trespassed, and then it was not with the idea of calling upon her.

'I could be dead, and he wouldn't care, apparently,' she told herself somewhat unreasonably, for to tell the truth she had rather enjoyed the latter of their encounters when pain was not required to be on the agenda.

While stripping down the gold wiring he had so meticulously woven on a previous occasion, he had been rather offensively inquisitive, or so she interpreted it.

'Are you engaged or anything, Dr French?'

When she could answer her words were darts of ice.

'Do you require such information for my treatment card, Mr McLeod?'

'Good lord, no!' It was so easy to silence her by shoving some instrument or other into her mouth. 'I was making polite conversation actually. It stands out a mile that you're not. I needn't have asked.'

Why did it stand out a mile? she asked herself, mortified. She would have to ask before she could rest. Given another opportunity to speak she said, 'You think that when one is engaged—or anything—one carries an unmistakable brand mark, do you?'

His smile was unbearably superior.

'Whatever it is, you haven't got it, Doctor.'

He turned away to dispose of the amalgam in his hand.

'That's all you know,' she said, schoolgirlishly, 'and I'm not prepared to discuss my affairs with any Tom, Dick or Harry.'

'It's a subject you seem loth to drop,' he said tiredly. 'I'm sorry I mentioned it now. I couldn't care less whether you're engaged, married, divorced or simply discarded; you go down in my records as female and perfect. In each case the reference is dental.'

She glared at him as she stood up.

'You don't even *try* not to be rude,' she accused him. 'If I were a psychologist I would say you're running away from a woman—or women—and taking it out on me!'

He looked aghast for a moment.

'That's absolutely untrue,' he protested, but he was not smiling. 'I have never taken anything out on you. You were at my throat from the start.'

'Because I objected to your kissing me on our first meeting? What should I have done to win your approval? Asked for more?'

'To win my approval you should have refused my invitation to call, being a woman. I imagined the doctor being a real old blue-nosed Robinson Crusoe, and certainly not a female. When I saw you dressed as Innocence, in plaits and jeans, and swigging neat whisky like a veteran, I thought I was expected to come up to scratch. Sorry if I was out of step, but that's the way it looked to me. Somebody should have told you the facts of life earlier, Dr French.'

Her bosom was rising and falling quickly, with anger and emotion.

'The only facts of life I cared about at that time, Mr McLeod, were innocuous enough. Your house had been occupied by a gentleman in whose company I had felt welcome and safe from molestation. I was prepared to extend my trust—and equal friendship—to you. As to my swigging neat whisky like a veteran, I've never tasted the stuff before, nor have had any desire to know it better since. You—and whisky—I find equally obnoxious to my palate. Need I see you again about this wretched tooth?'

There was a long pause while he fumbled a few papers together.

'No,' he said, as tense as she was. 'I shouldn't think there'll be any more trouble. If there is, do be sensible and let me know about it. Otherwise we can part—enemies.'

'No,' she said quickly. 'Being enemies sounds too active. I don't want to know of your existence, for my part.'

Now his smile was back and he bowed politely.

'Some things just *are* active by their very nature, Dr French. Have you tried to tell a volcano to stop erupting, or a typhoon to cease blowing? Are you another Canute . . . ?'

At this point she had stalked out, only to find Miss Huong on the other side of the exit door. She had obviously been listening, and had heard every word.

'Will you be coming again, Dr French?' she asked without batting an eyelid in embarrassment at being caught in such a position. She was a lovely girl, and looked her best in the satin cheongsam she favoured for evenings.

'In case you didn't hear, no,' Helen said bluntly, and blundered out into the darkness, biting her teeth once more in a way likely to do herself new damage.

That was some weeks ago, which should have pleased her well enough, but she found it aggravating wondering where he was and what he was doing. Not knowing—the uncertainty of everything—kept her nerves alerted and on edge.

Occasionally news of him reached her via her patients. Even the headman of the community, who came to her with a whitlow after smashing his thumb with a stone, spoke of him at length.

Sahib McLeod had honoured him and his family by joining them at supper last evening. He wanted to know what the Fan-Choans ate, and that was the best way of finding out, wasn't it? Sahib McLeod had sung Britis' song to entertain them, and this had made much laugh. Sahib McLeod was good fisherman. Did Memsahib Doctor know that? He sat many hours in little boat and fished with a stick. Some folk called him Hasra-lal, which—as Memsahib knew—meant Big Fish in the Fan-Choan language. He fished most days very early morning, before sun 'eat um'.

It was rather odd that Helen should wake at five the next morning and find herself so alert that further sleep was out of the question. As the first rays of the sun broke over the horizon, she was stepping down to the beach wearing a white towelling wrap over her bathing costume. Her hair was hanging loosely, gently lifted by a faint, thin breeze which was as yet too cool to be real.

Helen was halfway out of her wrap before she affected to be surprised by the dinghy bobbing at anchor about two hundred yards from the shore.

'I—I say—!' she called, and Geoff McLeod turned questioningly. 'Good morning! Do you mind if I have a dip here?'

'Good morning, and go ahead!' he invited. 'Why should I mind?'

'I thought perhaps the fish would be disturbed . . . ?'

'They're that already,' he explained, and pointed into the ether. 'Shouting disturbs the sound-waves and they react.'

'Oh.' She looked contrite. 'I'm very sorry.'

This time he merely waved his hand airily and she had no recourse but to swim. Whenever she broke surface and looked towards the dinghy there was only a broad, bush-shirted back to be seen. Her aquatic prowess was as lost on him as her feminine attractions, apparently, and it was simply because she resented being completely ignored that she swam out nearer and nearer to the boat. She was not the strongest of swimmers and knew it would take her all her time to get back to the beach, and it was at that moment she saw the spongy, poisonous mass, known as the Portuguese man o' war, floating ominously towards her.

'Get away!' she suddenly panicked, thrashing the water. 'Get away, you horrible creature!'

Geoff McLeod, who had—apparently—been taking a nap under his broad-brimmed panama hat, now turned irritably to observe her.

'Must you make so much din?'

'Don't you see what *that* is? It's coming for me! Help me! You . . . you . . . !'

Geoff took an oar from its rowlock and caught the stinger a stout slap so that it disintegrated into a horrid mass.

'Now go away!' he said irritably, and stared.

She had gone.

He glanced shorewards, looking for the cleaving of her arms in the water, but there was no sign of them.

Just then, he caught a pale reflection in the water near his boat and a few bubbles broke surface.

'Good lord . . . !'

He was over the side in an instant, grabbing the pale hair of the head which was once again sinking like a stone. As he lifted his burden into the dinghy, he saw that there was no time to lose, and, tossing the anchor in after her, he began to swim, dragging the dinghy towards the shore.

Fortunately she was not entirely water-logged and was soon breathing normally, though her eyes looked frightened still, as she opened them and beheld him.

'I was drowning—' she said faintly.

'You're all right now,' he told her firmly, 'so don't dwell on the might-have-been. Thank heaven I was there to get you out!'

She didn't tell him that if he hadn't been there in the first place neither would she.

'I think I'm all right,' she said, sitting up, suddenly acutely conscious of her lack of attire.

'Shock,' he said, putting her wrap clumsily about her shoulders. 'You're as likely to be shocked as anybody else. Go home and drink hot tea, then lie down for an hour. You hear?'

'Who's the doctor here?' she asked, trying to make her tone light. 'I must thank you, Mr McLeod,' she added more seriously.

'Whatever for?'

'My—my life, I suppose. It seems the balance between us is rather heavy on one side. You save my tooth—then my life. I suppose I must do something for you next.'

'Don't dramatise, Dr French. You'd have been washed up on the beach all right in a matter of minutes. In any case I can't think of anything you could do to help me. I'm invariably as fit as a fiddle, so don't expect to be called out in the middle of the night to a death-bed scene. I must go and change. Hadn't *you* better . . . ?'

She was drawing the scene out, she knew, and felt suddenly angry at the rebuff.

'Yes. Thanks again, anyway.'

She stalked off without a backward glance, and it was

only when she reached her own bedroom that her limbs began to tremble as though she had an ague and she called urgently for the hot tea 'Doctor' McLeod had prescribed for her.

Under the sheets, feeling warmer, she still brooded darkly.

'I asked for it and got it. Why did I have to see him when I loathe him so much? I must be becoming a glutton for punishment. The affair with Edward has made me expect to be hurt and despised. Have I no pride?'

CHAPTER EIGHT

For the first time in nearly three and a half years Helen French felt lonely in her remote appointment.

The Medical Committee back in Madras had pointed out to her the possibility of such a contingency occurring when she had first applied. It was a comparatively new appointment, they told her, but had always been filled by a male physician.

'Why shouldn't a man be lonely too?' she had asked reasonably. 'Women doctors are comparatively new as well and the appointment appeals to me immensely. For one thing I'm studying for my membership and there'll be opportunities for plenty of work—I think you'll agree with me there, gentlemen—and I can also gather all the information I require to write a thesis on Albinism in humans. I would like to be very seriously considered . . .'

Not many qualified doctors were of the same mind, apparently, and she got the appointment, together with a house and such furnishings as were necessary, a personal bearer (who could be trusted to guard his charge with his life if necessary), a medical orderly and a trained nurse. Local leave of three weeks was granted every six months, and there was assured contact with the mainland at least once a month when the mail-boat called.

Sometimes other craft dropped anchor out of curiosity. Once a barque, in full sail, anchored in the lee of the main island during a squall. The crew looked a piratical lot, and all the Fan-Cho males became warriors overnight and kept watch on the beach so that nothing should disappear and no throats be slit while they slept.

Another time, a clean-cut diesel motor-yacht called to use the islands as a backcloth to a film. Helen was required to treat a very handsome male star for sunstroke, which prevented her from taking him seriously as a hero at all. The final disillusionment came when this same gentleman, who had posed the body beautiful on thousands of glossy magazines all over the world, ordered the cameraman to 'shoot' his arrival on the beach—out of the sea—without showing his feet in close-up.

'I simply can't stand that sand between ma toes any longer!' he petulantly complained. 'Ah'm bein' washed up in ma shoes, dang it, or not at all!'

After the first six months the nurse, a Pakistani girl, had felt the call of home and left for Karachi. Others had been sent but had never settled. Sister Charmian Kaye, from the European Hospital in Madras, had done three months' duty and almost expired with boredom. But there was really no need of a nurse, for the women of Fan-Cho were intelligent enough to be able to look after their sick, when necessary. Helen had instructed the local midwife to hospital standards, and no pagan practices were tolerated here: they had really taken to asepsis in a big way, and Helen hesitated to put her foot down when she discovered that the women of the islands, being used to heady and intoxicating flower scents, had fallen in a big way for the smell of the antiseptic fluid in common use and were using it for every purpose under the sun apart from the cooking pot!

Perhaps it was because there was so little to do in her professional capacity that she found time to be lonely, or it might have been caused by the vacuum created in her life by Edward's departure.

In her heart she refused to blame him for anything: no crime had in fact been committed, for the simple reason that there was actually nothing between them. And yet there had been everything—in her own view.

'*I'm* at fault,' she insisted during these periods of heart-searching. 'I mistook an innocent, mild flirtation for love. I simply didn't know the difference. Perhaps I shall never know now, because I'll be afraid of it happening again.'

Her brushes with Geoff McLeod had been stimulating, exciting . . . and yet she could scarcely tell him of his effect upon her.

'Please come to dinner. I'm in the mood to enjoy a quarrel with you,' she joked as she fingered through her text-books during one period of study, thus showing her mind wasn't upon Dr Fergus's treatise on *Skeletal Types and their proneness to Typical Deformities and Diseases*. 'I'd look well sending a message like that to *him*. And yet he probably has a sense of humour tucked away somewhere.'

A din from the direction of the beach sent Bahadur down to investigate. He never needed telling to drop whatever he happened to be doing and dash off to join in any fun or squabble or excitement which happened to be afoot. People were to him what books were to his mistress: he read, enjoyed or derided people, and would squat on the outskirts of the Fan-Cho crowd either grinning or applauding or scowling darkly, but he was an accepted figure after more than three years and sometimes his opinion was sought when there was an argument, at which time he would darkly consider and then either shake or nod his head with exceeding and unmistakable vigour.

After half an hour Bahadur returned to his duties wearing a big smile.

The memsahib wasn't happy today? Well he had something to cheer her up. A dirty tramp steamer bound from Madras to Bengal had dropped off some mail. A whole bagful for Memsahib. Didn't that please her eyes? Even he had a letter from his wife telling him their eldest son had passed his examinations to go to college. Wasn't that something? Bahadur the bearer's son to go to college! Even a sweeper's brat might one day become Prime Minister.

Helen congratulated him, though not quite convinced about the emancipation of the Indian to such a degree. If Bahadur now nursed a dream of *his* son becoming Prime Minister, however, who was she to disillusion him?

She retired to her bed for the afternoon with her mail, feeling thrills of excitement as she untied the string binding the bundle of letters together. Firstly she glanced desultorily through the pile, noting the private letters from the brochures, etc. With a small child's preoccupation for leaving the best of a meal until the last she started on the less interesting communications first.

There was a shoe catalogue and a pamphlet informing her of a long past sale at a store in Knightsbridge, then the usual communications from various drug-houses, some with places where the customs' officers had neatly nipped off the free samples of new preparations, and finally Helen reached the letters.

She was a good correspondent herself and so had kept in touch with her closest friends of medical school days. Josie Warren—married now, and almost a mother, was full of her physical troubles, but Helen read patiently through two pages of these before Josie decided to change the subject.

'How's your love affair going, dear? When are *you* going to commit yourself to marriage? Believe me—

with all my present woes—I wouldn't have one moment of my married life unlived. I sometimes think I
never really existed before I met Bryan, and yet I had
studied and qualified and was practising, my head and
hands full and spilling over with knowledge, and yet
knowing nothing—absolutely nothing—about what I
now realise is a woman's only true and perfect voca-
tion.'

'All unmarried females should go and shoot themselves, according to Josie,' Helen pondered drily, and
read on.

'. . . You haven't mentioned Edward in your last two
letters. Don't tell me you've quarrelled? You barely
spoke of anything else before; he had either been
paying one of his visits or had written or sent you a
present. Now you're back to describing the palm trees
and some woman's twins and sign yourself inscrutably
as "Yours in haste". Please produce Edward at once. I
can't bear to think you won't be going through my
misery yourself before very much longer . . .'

'Evidently Josie missed Edward's engagement notice
in the papers,' she thought acidly as she put the letter
back in its envelope. 'I suppose somebody's expressing
sympathy in this lot.'

She fingered through the as yet unopened letters. One
from her surgeon friend, Alice Hughes, who at least
wasn't likely to be having a baby. Alice was a militant
feminist who thought of man's place in the world as a
well-trained dog's. Down, Rover! Another was from her
godmother, who had been her mother's friend. 'Aunt'
Lucia, as she called her, wrote amusing letters which
were like pocket editions of the weekly page she wrote

for a well known women's magazine. Aunt Lucia mixed with the top-drawer members of Society as easily as she breathed: she referred familiarly to countesses and their offspring as Vi and Pammy.

'Little Letty Higgs—(you know, Lord Amersham's fourth)—has fallen off her pony and fractured something or other. She's in plaster, anyhow, and looked most uncomfortable when I saw her in the Clinic, which is some satisfaction to me when I think of the time she deliberately spilled the lemonade all over me and then stuck out her horrid little tongue when compelled to apologise.'

The last letter was from—yes, it was from Edward!

Helen's heart beat faster as she stared at the small, practically undecipherable handwriting. What had Edward to say? Was he—apologising?

She felt she couldn't bear the suspense and yet she hesitated to slit the envelope.

Before she could do so, Bahadur appeared looking distraught. She read his fingers anxiously, and then nodded and put her mail—with Edward's unopened letter—on her bedside table.

Benji-hadad, the son of Ram, the pearl fisher, was lying seriously injured at the foot of the tallest tree on the island. He had fallen sixty feet to the ground from the coconut-bristling apex.

Feverishly Helen pulled on her clothes and hastened out into the compound where Vikrit was waiting with her bag and some splints all ready. Bahadur and a third man were carrying a collapsible stretcher.

'Let's hope something will be of use!' was Memsahib Doctor's prayer as she plunged into the dappled shadow of the trees.

CHAPTER NINE

BENJI-HADAD was the island palm-tree expert. It was his job in the communal life of Fan-Cho, for the palm-tree played a large part in everybody's existence.

There were three varieties of palm on the mother island, for four square miles of the total of six was composed of rain-forest entirely hemmed in by palms, which had their root-hold in the sandy subsoil of the extremity. The palmyra palm was bled of a substance from which toddy, the native beer, was made, and this was also useful for providing thatching for roofs and stems for palisades to keep the goats from becoming too venturesome: the areca palm was tall and beautiful, though of less domestic use than the other and therefore somewhat despised by the islanders. The coconut palm, however, was worth its weight in gold, for not only did it provide toddy from its leathery leaves and an edible nut, but the milk from inside the nut was collected, fermented and distilled into arrack, a potent spirit which was used on all festive occasions, and—Helen suspected—had a few festive occasions created specially in its honour.

Va-tu's approaching marriage to Kali, the brother of Simbat-lal, was no doubt responsible for Benji-hadad's occupation on this day, for there was a heap of coconuts in an old sack bearing the legend 'granulated sugar' near his crumpled, broken body.

His scream as he fell had drawn a group of horrified children to the scene, and they, in turn, had run for their

59

mothers, who now moaned and wrung their hands in typical gestures of hopelessness and despair. Benji's own mother was howling like a mad thing, and had to be restrained, but fortunately nobody had touched the lad. He lay prone, his head grotesquely on one side. The impact from his fall, on dusty sand, had covered him with particles so that his body glinted as though phosphorescent.

Helen sought the pulse first. It still fluttered weakly, and she felt a surge of relief followed by a moment's utter panic. If he had been dead, it would have been tragically simple, but that glimmer of life must be nurtured, and how many fractures the lad must have sustained she didn't dare imagine!

She accepted the appearance of the bush-shirted figure near her as she knelt as a right and natural thing as she began her examination of the splayed limbs. One foot lay distorted, almost the wrong way round, and the leg was considerably foreshortened.

'It's a mess, isn't it?' she asked in a peculiar matter-of-fact voice she scarcely recognised as her own.

'Pretty grim,' said Geoff McLeod. 'I don't know much about anything from the neck downwards, but do let me know if I can help.'

'This is my first major accident in three years,' she confided, 'and one gets rusty. I'm afraid of overlooking anything.'

'You're doing fine.'

Finally Helen made her report.

'I should say he fell more or less on his feet and dropped over to the left. There's a little concussion, but no fracture that I can find—to the skull or to the shoulders. His left arm is fractured at the wrist, but that's simple enough. The main shock was taken by the left leg, and I don't know just how seriously the iliac has been impacted into the pelvis. There may be internal injuries to watch out for, but my first concern is to get him back to my house and on an examination couch. Unfortunately our stretcher is a sling and everything will joggle. That could be bad.'

'Shall I get a hard litter organised for him?'

'There isn't time. If he's bleeding I want to know about it without any more ado.'

'Well we'll firm up your existing stretcher as much as possible.'

Geoff McLeod sent everybody scattering looking for driftwood, and as soon as Helen and Vikrit had strapped the injured boy to long splints, the stretcher was a criss-cross of pieces of firm timber.

'Ready!'

In a foursome they lifted Benji on to the stretcher and it was borne away, Helen following, wiping the sweat out of her eyes and wondering if—or rather hoping—she was dreaming all this.

More than an hour later she was scrubbed up and acting surgeon, while Vikrit shared the honours of assisting at a major operation with McLeod sahib. Two of the islanders, men who had been working inshore fishing for prawns, had been called in to use their strength in pulling Benji's impacted hip joint back into the fractured socket, and as there were internal injuries Helen had no recourse but to make an abdominal incision and see what they were.

'The intestine is torn and there's some fluid in the peritoneum,' she announced, 'but it's not as bad as I thought. Keep that saline moving, Bahadur,' she said sharply, 'and change it for the blood in fifteen minutes, the way I showed you. I'm going to stitch the intestine, swab out the cavity and dust everything with penicillin.'

'Well done!' said Geoff McLeod when at last she had finished and sutured the wound. 'Can I put the dressing on? You must be exhausted.'

'Thank you. Now there's the plastering,' she said mechanically. 'We haven't finished yet.'

The hips and the right leg were enclosed in plaster bandages, and still she didn't crack, though she had never put in such an afternoon's work in her life. She even found a reserve of energy to plaster the fractured wrist, carefully folding the hand at the knuckles so that it wouldn't grow rigid.

'Now put him on the veranda bed,' she instructed, and Benji, the men still holding the plastered leg, was transferred to the wire-netting-covered area of the veranda that had been prepared with an emergency (though of a less severe nature) in mind.

Geoff McLeod proved himself to be inventive when it came to providing some means of traction for the plastered limb to relieve the two men, who, naturally, were tiring by now.

Benji was strapped firmly to the hard mattress and then his leg was raised and stretched by the means of a stout rope and an iron chest in which Helen kept her documents.

'I think that's all we can do for him,' she then announced, removing the soaking turban from her hair. 'We'll just have to hope for the best.'

'All?' asked Geoff McLeod incredulously. 'You've done blinking wonders, woman!'

She looked at him uncomprehendingly. Now that all was over she felt strangely lightheaded.

'He isn't out of the wood yet, you know.'

'I do know. But if there's anything needed to get him out, I'm confident you'll do it. Will you shake hands, Dr French?'

She tried to laugh, suddenly conscious of her steaming hair and sweat-soaked gown.

'I'll shake hands, Mr McLeod,' she tried to say lightly, 'but there's really no need to think you have to be friends or anything. I simply did my job, as you're doubtless doing yours all the time.'

'You did three fully-grown men's jobs for a time there, my girl; doctor, surgeon and orthopaedist, not to mention the improvisation necessary. Most surgeons have a hospital and qualified assistants.'

'I think *my* assistants deserve some credit. Thank *you* especially, Mr McLeod.'

Bahadur arrived and fluttered that tea—very strong tea—was waiting in the living-room.

'I must stay here and watch my patient,' Helen said automatically. 'When his pulse improves I'll feel happier. You go and have some tea, Mr McLeod. I'll have my cup here.'

'Yes, there's the nursing,' he said, without heeding her instructions. 'You can't do much more without relief or you'll crack.'

'One doesn't talk of cracking,' Helen said shortly. 'It's my job, Mr McLeod. Please understand that.'

'Yes, well, please forgive me if I have only just now realised how much of a job it is for a woman. Most women I've known would have swooned at first sight of the scene back there. I can't get over the way you sailed into it—almost taking everything in your stride. But before I become ridiculous in my efforts to show my sincere admiration, may I suggest something which might help?'

'Go ahead.'

Helen began to gulp the hot tea Bahadur had placed on the veranda rail beside her.

'Miss Huong is—or rather was—a trained nurse. I

would like to offer her services to you—nights, shall we say?'

'What about Miss Huong? Do you—er—normally offer her services without consulting her?'

He decided to ignore the acid in the query.

'I think I can safely say she'd do it for me.'

Ah, yes, Helen thought. Wild-Blossom Huong would do it for Mr Wonderful McLeod.

'Thank you,' she said coldly, 'but I wouldn't like to trouble anyone else. So far it has all been splendid, but now I'll manage somehow. I can get a woman in, you know.'

'An *untrained* woman, I suppose,' he said grimly. 'However, have it your way. I was thinking of the lad.'

'So am I. Miss Huong might be thinking too much of you!'

Now it was out. Now he would be angry with her.

'Good lord!' he said, as though he was seeing her for the first. 'Good lord! You don't imagine Blossom has any feeling for me personally, do you?'

'It had crossed my mind,' Helen confessed.

'Good lord!' he said again, in absolute wonderment. 'Women are the very devil. They get an absolutely cock-eyed idea and sit on it, like a hen on an egg. I can't think of anything more fantastic than Blossom and me. You should hear her swear at me in Chinese! However, I don't expect you're in a mood to be influenced. Can I do anything more for you?'

'No, thank you.'

'Right. I'll keep in touch.'

He turned and was gone, leaving her at once lonely and nettled.

Wasn't he sensitive to the fact that Blossom Huong hated her—Helen French—breathing the same air as her employer? Perhaps a Chinese girl's love was as undemonstrative as the rest of her emotions, but one was driven into the belief that what found no outward expression must ferment the more within.

'She hates me,' Helen pondered, 'and she'll do something about it before we've all finished on Fan-Cho. It's rather like waiting for a snake to strike.'

Helen shivered involuntarily, and decided she was suffering belatedly from shock.

CHAPTER TEN

At nine p.m. Benji suddenly took a turn for the worse. His pulse flickered and almost died, and for a moment Helen considered opening the chest and massaging the heart to life again.

'You can't die after all, boy!' she cried out frenziedly. 'Come on, now! Come on! *You* make an effort.'

Of course she couldn't subject him to further surgery, she realised almost at once. He was already shocked to the limit of his endurance. Coming out of unconsciousness into great pain was one factor: he probably didn't understand what was happening and would submit fatalistically like the rest of his kind, rather than fight for his existence.

Helen injected both pethidine and adrenalin, and soon she felt the pulse revive and beat in quickening impulses until the worst of the threat was over for the time being.

Bahadur had put a wicker-work chaise-longue beside the boy's bed for her to relax on, and she had told Vikrit to come and relieve her at three a.m. Every hour which passed was one in their favour, and she would feel happier if at this hour tomorrow night there was still the anxiety of the night hours lying ahead of them.

'Excuse me,' came a voice into her thoughts. 'Dr French, I have come to help you.'

Helen looked up, half wondering if she was distrait enough to be having hallucinations. A nurse was standing at the veranda door calmly removing her dark cloak and revealing a starched blue dress beneath a snowy apron. A crisp, jaunty cap rose from jet-black, smooth shining hair which crowned a pale, olive-skinned female face.

Inscrutable, black oriental eyes, only slightly elongated, looked from doctor to patient as though absorbing the scene before action was decided upon.

'Miss Huong—!' Helen gasped. 'I told Mr McLeod' there was no need for you to bother . . . it's most unfair of him . . .'

'The decision to come was entirely mine, Dr French, I assure you,' the newcomer said coolly. 'I wouldn't be here if my heart wasn't in it. If you want me to stay, I'll stay, and if not, I'll go.'

Take me or leave me, she might have said, and Helen was half inclined to leave her from the outset.

'Well . . .' she hesitated, playing for time. 'As you see, it's a bad do. There's the drip to watch and the catheter to measure, and check, besides the normal things like pulse and respirations . . .'

'I *am* fully qualified, Dr French,' said the Chinese girl, and took a step, as though magnetised, towards the bed. She bent and put her cheek close to the parted, pale lips of Benji-hadad.

'He breathes in sleep,' she suddenly announced, smiling in sudden excitement. 'He will get better with good nursing.'

She looked suddenly at Helen as though having revealed more of herself than she had intended. Noticeably her smile faded.

'Well, Dr French?' she asked coldly.

'Whatever she feels for me she'll be a good help with Benji,' Helen suddenly decided, feeling happier.

'I'll be glad if you'll take on the case, Nurse Huong,' she said formally, 'and it's extremely kind of you. Won't it interfere with your work for Mr McLeod?'

'Not unduly. The oriental has learned how to survive on the minimum of everything the occidental gluttons on. Don't you agree, Dr French? We eat less, sleep less, need less to make us happy and contented.'

Helen yawned, irrepressibly, watching the girl check Benji's inert form under the bedclothes before professionally tucking him in.

'I wouldn't know, Nurse. I would like to glutton an hour or two away if you think you can manage?'

'Oh, *I* can manage, thank you. I'll prepare a report and you can read it when I've finished my spell of duty. Naturally I'll call you if there should be any deterioration in the patient's condition.'

'Naturally,' said Helen, feeling herself to be dismissed.

She stood her ground, however, for a few seconds longer.

'I've prepared an injection of pethidine which you may give him at one a.m., Nurse, or when he grows restless. Do you understand?'

'Of course I understand, Dr French.' The girl sounded offended.

'I'm sorry,' said Helen, hastily, 'I'm not used to having someone helping me with such a command of English as you have, Nurse Huong. I find it preferable to emphasise an instruction rather than it should be misinterpreted.'

'With me you needn't worry about misinterpretation, Dr French. We Chinese are occasionally subjected to education, you know. I myself finished with the equivalent of a BA at the University of Nanking.'

Helen now felt that whatever she said in reply would be construed as being either patronising or flippant. She hoped Nurse and Benji had a good night and almost staggered off to her own room, glad to escape the almost tangible resentment the Chinese girl showed towards her.

'She and I should have a girlish chat one day,' she pondered as she undressed. 'When she knows there's not a hope of Geoff McLeod and me coming closer to a romance than calling the dogs off one another she may see things a little clearer than she does at present. I don't understand her attitude. Really, I don't. She's heard us at one another's throats more than once . . .' She crept beneath the mosquito netting, finding her limbs aching from past tensions as she eased and stretched them.

'I wonder if that's the way they make love in China?' was her final, sleepy thought.

It was lunchtime next day, and Benji was still holding his own, when Helen recollected Edward's letter and sought it in vain.

Merciful heaven . . . ! Where could it be?

'Bahadur!' she called sharply, and as the bearer appeared with a bowl of curried prawns and rice, 'have you been tidying up again? Where's my mail? I haven't read it all yet.'

Bahadur indicated the pile of brochures and other correspondence lying neatly on the desk.

'There was a letter. An unopened letter. You find it instantly!'

Bahadur became offended, snapping his speaking fingers together with his flashing eyes to indicate this.

Such a letter was under Memsahib's pillow at this very moment. He stalked off to get Edward's letter and placed it before her. Always Memsahib kept letters written by that same gentleman under her pillow. He, Bahadur, only thought he was doing right, having recognised the writing.

'Well, thank you, Bahadur,' she said more kindly, 'and it was very sweet of you to remember and be so thoughtful.'

The servant still eyed her coldly.

'I'm sorry. We've had a bad twenty-four hours, all of us, and I'm still tired.'

Bahadur replied that a pukka sahib never kicked his dog when he was upset, nor a pukka memsahib her bearer.

'You'll have me crying in a moment,' Helen threatened, and the servant forgave her quickly, with an outsize grin to show it. She wished there was some concrete way to prove her affection, but was also aware of the line he drew between them as mistress and man.

He liked talking about his wife and family, however, and occasionally about himself.

'Bahadur,' she said, in genuine enquiry, 'were you born without speech?'

He became positively loquacious as she politely ignored Edward's letter, forked her curry into her mouth and watched attentively.

On the contrary, he had learned to speak with his mouth before other children. He had been a fine, sturdy and precocious youngster. (Bahadur did not use the word 'precocious', but that was the gist of it.) As a young man he had sung and danced in the temples for the tourists, but as he didn't consider this an existence suitable to his manhood, he had joined the Army and worked his way up to Subadar major. That was a good life, a man's life, and he had seen almost the whole of India, as a result of his army service. Unfortunately, when the white sahibs were asked to leave India things weren't so good, and bombs were thrown about everywhere; not only where there was real soldier fighting, but in the market-places, everywhere and anywhere. A bomb had fallen near his house, and though all the family had scrambled free of the wreck of their dwelling he—the father—had found himself unable to speak. He had been to hospital, had many doctors look in his mouth, but they all said the same. Has tongue, has little box in throat like other men, but nothing come. No noise. They shake their heads and say wait. He—Bahadur—had waited fifteen years, but (he shrugged) no different, and now it didn't matter. He could talk with fingers and he was a great man for thinking a lot. Didn't Memsahib Doctor agree that one couldn't think while one was talking?

Helen smiled and nodded.

But (Bahadur continued his life story relentlessly), he had taken a fancy to medical men and their habits. They were all good sahibs and memsahibs, too, and having become bearer to one doctor, he had continued in the medical service, though his wife, who was still in the north, hadn't given him a child in ten years and thought him somewhat neglectful of her.

Feeling this monologue might go on indefinitely now that Bahadur had got into his stride, Helen politely suggested she have her coffee on the veranda, and stood up looking pointedly at Edward's letter in her hand. She had no sooner settled down in a reclining chair on the veranda, however, than a visitor arrived at the bungalow looking distinctly hot and put out.

'Mr McLeod!' Helen exclaimed, wondering why her heart should act peculiarly at this interruption. 'Is anything wrong?'

'No. Why should there be?' he asked, with a somewhat forced smile, mopping his brow with a large, snowy handkerchief and sinking into another chair near her. 'How's the boy?'

'Much improved. His pulse is still weak but steadier,

and he's sleeping a good deal without drugs. We may get him fairly all right eventually.'

'Can he be moved on to the *Madrassi Belle*, do you think?'

'Why? Is the *Madrassi Belle* due?'

'Didn't you know?'

Helen sighed.

'I didn't get my most important mail read yet.' She put Edward's letter into her skirt pocket. 'But I suppose the ship *is* due. A month's gone, hasn't it?'

'Yes. We've known each other a month,' he announced as Bahadur arrived with the coffee and went to get another cup. 'I bet outsiders just won't believe we're still "Mister" and "Doctor" to each other after a month.'

Helen looked at her visitor in some consternation. He was smiling awkwardly and was still obviously ill at ease.

'What did you want to see me about, Mr McLeod?' she asked distinctly.

'I want you to call me Geoff,' he said as clearly, 'and I want to call you Helen—when we meet, of course.'

'Of course,' she said suspiciously. 'But why, all of a sudden?'

'Just that it sounds more human and friendly and doesn't commit us in any way.'

Helen pondered as she poured his coffee.

'I can't help thinking there's something behind all this, Mr McLeod,' she said suddenly. 'What is it? Is this the olive branch or the hand of friendship you're offering . . . ?'

'Well, actually, I wanted to ask a favour of you.'

'Ah!' she nodded wisely. 'Proceed. There's no need for anything but to ask it. I'm already physically in your debt, you remember?'

'It's a favour I can't ask unless we're less formal with

each other,' he said somewhat irritably. 'There's someone coming to see me on the *Madrassi Belle*. I suppose you'll have visitors too. I wondered if you'd be hostess for me at evening dinner, if you'd even offer hospitality to my guest. She's a woman, you see.'

'I see,' Helen said crisply.

Geoff McLeod's face flushed dully red.

'I don't think you *do* see,' he contradicted her. 'I'm simply asking you to help me out because there are no facilities at my place. I've turned my house into a surgery and it would be inconvenient to sling all my equipment out for one evening's entertainment.'

Helen looked at him calmly.

'All right, Geoff,' she said quietly, 'there's no need to go into explanations or raise your hackles any further. My Super will be coming and you and your friend are welcome to join us as a matter of course. I hope your friend won't mind sharing my bedroom . . . there's only the one.'

'That's very good of you . . .' he lowered his gaze.

'And of course call me Helen,' she added finally. 'We've been rather stiff and silly all this month, when you think of it, and, as you say, using Christian names doesn't commit us in any other way.'

The grey eyes looked sincerely into the clear blue, and for the first time she noticed how long and dark his eyelashes were, so lost on a man.

'Thank you—Helen,' he said rather shyly, and offered his hand. 'I don't think my friend realises what an out-of-the-way place Fan-Cho is. Her name is Celeste— a lovely name, isn't it?—Celeste Vandenburg. She's very pretty. Different from you—you know?' her eyebrows rose as she smiled somewhat wryly. 'She's a brunette.'

CHAPTER ELEVEN

AT long last Helen felt she could settle down to read the letter (which was now burning a hole in her pocket) without further interruption.

Benji-hadad was maintaining his improvement and, having been told in detail what had happened to him, he was adopting the philosophical, fatalistic attitude of most Asians to personal tragedy and inconvenience, and could be guaranteed not to fidget or become bored with his condition. He would, in fact, only have to be watched lest he be willing to bear more pain than he was expected to do, for Helen knew that fortitude, even in the very young, was as inbred as their closeness to nature.

The one thing Benji became argumentative about was the accident itself. People had told him he had fallen from the tree. This was absolute rubbish and lies, he said firmly in his own words, for although he didn't remember much about it himself he was convinced that the raffia lashing which he used to climb trees with, and was composed of a loose loop which held him in position and was fastened securely round one ankle, had broken as he was preparing to descend, and he wished everyone to know this and not cast reflections upon his prowess as a climber.

It did not occur to the lad to ask if he would ever be able to climb again, and Helen was glad of this, for she couldn't honestly have answered.

At the moment the shattered body was only held together by plaster of paris, and what was going on inside this shell it was impossible to tell, for Helen had no X-ray machine on the island.

She was anxious for news of the medical ship, the *Madrassi Belle*, hoping that the visiting supervisor would be able to tell her more of Benji's chances and perhaps take him off to hospital along with the throat cancer suspect.

Would that supervisor prove to be Edward?

She tore open the envelope nervously and withdrew two fairly closely written sheets of writing paper, which shook in her suddenly trembling hands.

'My dear Helen,' she read, 'my leave seemed end-less and you will never know how happy I am to be back again in harness and knowing you decided to stay on in my district. You do realise I daren't influence you one way or the other, don't you? Which is why I haven't contacted you before, though once or twice I had almost to manacle myself to prevent that same hand from writing Dear—Dearer—Dearest Helen . . . !'

Helen raised her head and blinked her eyes. No, she wasn't dreaming. There were bees busy in the bauhinias and purple emperor lilies, and a blowfly was banging itself against the netting of the veranda wall, shining green-blue in the sunlight. She read on, her heart thumping strangely.

'. . . I will be seeing you on Tuesday the fourth, D.V., and may then enlarge on such sentiments as I have been storing this long time. Have all your re-ports, etc., up to date so that we will have longer to spend in amicable converse. This much I will say, Helen, which I trust will please you—that the sophisticated ladies of London society can't hold a candle to you as far as I'm concerned.

'I've been asked to bring a visitor out for a Professor McLeod who is with you on Fan-Cho at present. She—the visitor—is hot stuff, if you like feminine mustard.

'Be seeing you,
'Edward.'

Helen read the letter again, feeling there must be something she had misread or omitted to read altogether. Edward hadn't mentioned his engagement, and the way he had written to her was in the old way, neither coolly nor passionately, but in familiar, flatteringly affectionate terms. Surely he wouldn't write such a letter and then tell her when they met that he was engaged to be married? This would not only be cruel, after all she had suffered already, but positively sadistic.

She rose and took a walk round the veranda, automatically looking in on Benji, and observing that he was sleeping under the influence of his noontime injection for pain.

Again she read Edward's letter.

It was as though things were exactly the same between them, and yet she wasn't entirely fooled. Supposing she had decided to leave Fan-Cho when her previous contract was concluded? What then? She would by now be back in England and Edward here, and she doubted he would be writing her in quite the same terms if she was six thousand miles distant from him. Also, why shouldn't he influence her decision to either go or stay? If he was fond of her one would imagine he would try to persuade her to remain near him, but he had seemed quite content to leave it to fate, and as fate had kept her on Fan-Cho he had accepted the throw of the dice as being in his favour while being none of his responsibility.

'Maybe I've allowed myself to become embittered,' she pondered darkly, 'but Edward's letter doesn't seem quite straight somehow. And what about the announcement in *The Times*? Could it have been somebody else bearing the same name?

'And a doctor holding the same degrees?' she asked herself silently. 'No! no! Edward and I have to talk as we've never talked before. I may not be able to hold a candle to sophisticated people, but I'm not a bumpkin either. I want to know the truth, whatever it is, and whether Edward loves me or not.'

It was with sudden dismay she recollected her promise to Geoff McLeod, to both house his lady friend and provide the main meals. This meant that she and Edward might find it difficult to have a heart-to-heart talk in the evening, for it would be too humiliating to have to obviously seek such an opportunity.

'Oh, damn Geoff McLeod!' she said with sudden heat. 'He's caused me nothing but trouble since he came to Fan-Cho!'

All day she wondered how she could get out of her promise, but there seemed no way other than to tell McLeod that she and the visiting medical superintendent were more than friends, and this was not strictly true as yet.

'And may never be if Edward thinks I'm treating him off handedly,' Helen fretted.

Ling John came along cheerfully that evening and presented his master's compliments saying that he had been instructed to discuss the following day's dinner menu with 'Mem'.

'I am good cook,' he bowed affably, displaying his long yellow teeth in a grin. 'Work long time in famous restaurant, Hong Kong.'

'Then you suggest a menu, Ling John,' Helen said readily, not wanting to think for herself.

'Suggest oysters, Mem. Plenty on island. Then excellent curry with chicken. Chicken also plentiful as Mem knows. This to be served with flied lice.'

Helen looked somewhat horrified for an instant.

'Oh!' she suddenly understood. '*Fried rice*. Why not boiled, Ling John?'

'Boiled lice food of China and India peasant, Mem. Flied lice much more nicer. After all, cook know best.' He smiled again to take the sting from the gentle reproof. 'After main dish suggest slice melon. Tongue ve'y hot after curry.'

Helen was by now utterly fascinated by the proposed menu, or rather by Ling John's lisping version of it. He could use the letter 'r' very well in some words and yet avoided it altogether in others or substituted the 'l'.

'I think that will do very nicely, Ling John,' she applauded. 'Just run through the items once more, will you?'

The Chinese did so, and then both became aware of a third party in the vicinity. It was Nurse Huong, come to take over night duty with Benji-hadad.

She addressed Ling John at some length in Cantonese, glancing occasionally in Helen's direction. What she said did not seem to please the servant, for his ready grin faded as he made a surly response and also looked at Helen with a glimmer of suspicion in his eyes.

'May I ask what you said to him?' Helen asked the newcomer, sharply.

'You may if you wish, Dr French,' Blossom Huong replied in her excellent English. 'I was telling this peasant here that you were laughing at him and not to make a fool of himself.'

'I think that was rather presumptuous of you, Nurse,' Helen said indignantly. 'I was not laughing at Ling John. I think his accent most attractive, and only wish I could speak Chinese as well as he does English. Also he is a most charming person, and your words belittled him far more than you realise. I'll see you tomorrow, Ling John,' she called clearly, 'and you shall cook while my man waits at table. Thank you for the menu, and goodnight.'

The boy went, and Blossom Huong looked forbiddingly at Helen lest she continue with her criticism.

They both went to see Benji-hadad and discussed the day's progress and the night's programme without more ado.

The motor-launch came chugging into the bay and the islanders danced with excitement as they waited for it to come within swimming distance. All the community was there, that is all except Min Hana, who had been holding morning surgery as usual when her patients had suddenly heard news of the arrival of the *Madrassi Belle* and dashed off, forgetful of their ailments. Even Hasralal— the big fish—was there on the beach, pacing up and down and pinching his already lean face still more as he attempted to whistle nonchalantly.

He was glad Helen had not seen fit to come down, for now that Celeste was so near he wanted to see her without somebody looking on to see how affected he might be. After all, he hadn't seen Celeste since she had hurled the ring back at him, telling him to go his 'damned way' but not to expect her to accompany him into obscurity. 'Obscurity' was Fan-Cho and his new assignment with the Government of India. She was an army nurse and would have preferred a fashionable wedding in Hong Kong and thereafter a leisured life with a nice house on the peak overlooking the harbour, but not within smelling distance of it.

Life was good for well-placed Europeans in the Far East: labour was cheap and plentiful and a beautiful woman had nothing to do other than pander to her beauty, dallying in hairdressing salons and beauty parlours and fashion houses, day, week and month long, never soiling her painted finger-nails or exerting herself beyond the minimum it took to do these things.

Celeste Vandenburg saw him the moment the launch was seized and dragged inshore. He was quite the most handsome man she had ever seen, and yet his masculinity was always offended if one told him so.

What was he thinking about her and this visit? That she had followed him deliberately, unable to release him from her life after all?

Would he kiss her?

Should she take the initiative and throw herself upon him?

Dr Courtenay was calling to a coloured boy to come and carry her through the surf. Why didn't Geoff do it? He was smiling at her, but still didn't save her from the indignity of being swept up by a native and dumped on the sand like a parcel.

'Geoffrey!' she then cried out with just the right amount of a break in her voice. 'Darling, I—!'

The islanders' shouts almost drowned her carefully rehearsed little speech.

'Min Hana!' they shrieked delightedly. 'Min Hana cum!'

Helen had decided to join the reception committee after all. She was flushed with hurrying and held out her hand to Edward Courtenay without acknowledging anyone else.

'Sorry I was late, sir,' she said formally. 'This is my surgery time.'

'Well done!' said Edward, as formally. 'Nothing like keeping to schedule, is there, Dr French?'

They both turned away and went up the beach together.

'Who's that?' Celeste asked thinly, forgetting her rehearsed lines.

'Who, Helen?' Geoff asked, deliberately casual. 'She's the doctor hereabouts. She's putting you up overnight.'

'Oh? That's very kind of her, isn't it?' Celeste asked. There had been no kiss and now Geoff was propelling her gently in the wake of the others. 'You're not exactly alone on your desert island, then?'

'No, not exactly,' he smiled. 'Helen was one of the surprises in store for me.'

'Pleasant?' asked Celeste, most unpleasantly.

'I wouldn't say that, exactly. Unexpected would be my word. Helen's always doing the unexpected. Do you know, the other day . . .'

Celeste, however, was not interested, and he smiled wryly and dropped the subject.

'There'll be iced tea up at the house,' he said instead, 'and then you'll meet Helen for yourself.'

'I can hardly wait,' said Celeste acidly.

CHAPTER TWELVE

'Do go ahead,' Helen invited hastily, stepping back from the dressing table with her hair loose about her shoulders. 'I'll use the mirror in the bathroom.'

'Don't go for a minute,' urged Celeste Vandenburg languidly. 'I seem to have intruded on your privacy without having a chance to get to know you. What with this rule about sleeping in the heat of the day and you being a working girl, we'll be saying goodbye before we know what's what.'

'I hope you did manage to sleep this afternoon?' Helen asked politely.

'Yes, thanks, like a log. Where did you get to?'

'Well, I have a patient on the veranda and Dr Courtenay and I were discussing him. If we can get him out to the *Madrassi Belle* he's going to hospital.'

Celeste draped herself at the dressing table in a negligée and began brushing her short, black hair. She was a striking-looking girl with tawny eyes and full, pouting lips which she outlined with orange-coloured lipstick. Her figure too was voluptuous, though her waist was positively tiny.

'Do we dress formally out here on Crusoe's isle?' she asked casually, fully aware that her companion had been eyeing her with feminine interest.

'Wrong hemisphere,' Helen now replied.

Celeste looked round sharply.

'What did you say?'

'I said Crusoe's island is reputedly on the other side of the world. Fan-Cho means the Isles of Nowhere, but

we're not so remote nowadays as the name implies.
We're even civilised enough to dress for dinner when
the occasion demands it—and, yes, I think this one
does.'

Celeste smiled blandly into the mirror.

'Sorry if I rubbed you up the wrong way, Dr French. I
didn't mean to poke fun at your little community.'

'That's all right. I'm not offended really. Anyway, you
should know that it's one of Geoff's fads to keep up
appearances. He would probably still dress for dinner if
he was the only person on the island.'

The atmosphere became ever so slightly refrigerated.
Celeste was now engaged in tweaking a few superfluous
hairs from her thinned eyebrows.

'Well, I don't know how intimately you know Geoff,
do I? I mean—'

'*Intimately*, Miss Vandenburg?' Helen questioned.

'I meant to say "friendly". I suppose you're pretty
friendly by now being the only Europeans on the island?
If I was in administration I would question the wisdom of
placing a man and a woman in such a position. There's
bound to be talk . . .'

'Talk, Miss Vandenburg?'

Celeste swung round on the rattan stool, looking her
most charming and understanding.

'You're questioning everything I say, Dr French, as
though I'm being deliberately offensive, or something.
Surely you know what the shore Europeans are like in
their clubs, having their sundowners? They have everybody's names linked in some scandal or other, often
without foundation. But you and Geoff . . .'

'You mean that here we have a solid foundation for
such a scandal?'

'That's what I do mean. Yes.'

Helen smiled grimly.

'They'd be surprised if they knew.'

'Knew what?'

'Oh, nothing . . .' Helen turned to make her way to the bathroom.

'*Dr French!*'

For a moment, as she turned in the doorway, Helen saw a flash in the tawny eyes which was not so friendly, but forgot it next moment as the honeyed tones embraced her.

'My dear, I think you're the sweetest little innocent; frightfully clever and all that at your job, but ignorant of the ways of this wicked world. I've been around more than you—Singapore, Hong Kong, Colombo—and believe me, I know people. I think—in all fairness to yourself—you should ask Geoff to leave. He just needs any old island, not this one particularly.'

'I don't understand you,' Helen said, a dull flush staining her cheeks.

Celeste professed sudden remorse.

'Oh, I'm sorry! What a clumsy fool I am! Maybe I'm forgetting something—that you care a little bit for Geoff, perhaps?'

Helen's flush deepened.

'I wouldn't have embarrassed you like this for the world!' Celeste almost gnashed her teeth in her eagerness to know the facts before she had her own private tête-à-tête with her ex-fiancé.

Helen swallowed her indignation like a bitter pill.

'I'm *not* embarrassed in the least, Miss Vandenburg,' she said at length, 'but I must admit to further lack of experience in discussing my private affairs with strangers. I know some women revel in that kind of thing, but I hope I never have time for it.'

This time she very resolutely made her departure, leaving Celeste seething with hatred.

'The little brat!' she almost spat. 'How dare she patronise me . . .! Oh!'

The last exclamation was torn from her as a figure appeared on the veranda and stood irresolute for a moment.

'Miss Vandenburg! You remember me?'

Celeste stared, not believing her eyes.

'Is that really you, Wild Blossom? Come in! What are you doing here?'

'In this house, or on this island?'

'Both.'

'I came with Mr McLeod as his secretary. Here I nurse the patient at nights. But what are *you* doing here? I hope you made it up, the quarrel?'

'No, not yet.' Here Celeste sighed. 'There's no privacy. I haven't seen Geoff since he dumped me here about noon. I share a room—everything—with this woman . . . this doctor. What do you know about her, Blossom?'

'Very little. She is efficient.'

'Does she see much of Geoff?'

'No. They do not like one another at first. Now, I think, a little better.'

Celeste sighed again.

'We must get him away from here, Wild Blossom. This is no life for him. He'll grow into one of those terrible bores who can only talk about their jobs. We had a good life in Hong Kong. Remember the parties we gave—how gay they were?'

'Yes, I do!' laughed Nurse Huong, her face unusually animated for an instant. 'But there is an old Chinese proverb which says, "A river never runs backwards to its source". What is over is done with, Miss Vandenburg.'

'That's true. But there could still be gay times ahead of us if we could all be together again. I was at fault, Wild

Blossom, I should never have returned Geoffrey's ring. You see, as things are, he is quite free to fall in love with somebody else, and when there's no competition the only woman on an island assumes attractions and attributes she may not really possess.'

'You mean Mr McLeod might fall in love with Dr French?' Nurse Huong smiled maliciously.

'It's not impossible, Blossom. She's quite pretty in a pale way.'

'I think she is a doll. A wax doll.'

'Such vehemence, Blossom! I take it you don't like her much either?'

Nurse Huong's bosom rose and fell quickly as she spoke.

'I have been taught to think in symbols. Dr French is the symbol of all I have wished to be, tried and worked to be, yet for her all goes well and for me there is frustration after frustration. I study in China, and because my parents have fled to Hong Kong and send me no money I am allowed no grants to take my examinations. I work as a nurse, but I wish to be a doctor, a *Communist* doctor if that is what they want, but they find out my brother has invested part of the family fortune in America. I am threatened with death, but they decide on expulsion instead. I go to Hong Kong, and when I tell the authorities I wish to continue my medical studies, they say "You are a Communist. You just arrive from China. Nothing doing." I would be starving if it was not for Mr McLeod who makes me his receptionist and then his secretary. He says, sympathetically, he teach me to be dentist instead of doctor if I will settle for that. I settled for that, and in two years I may qualify and practise, but every time I see Dr French, hear a medical term come from her lips, I feel evil and resentment inside me. Why should life be so damned hard for only some of us?'

'Poor Blossom!' Celeste said softly, her hand outstretched to squeeze the other's shoulder. 'Some people do seem to get all the lifts, don't they? If she gets Geoff you may even be done out of your dentistry.'

Nurse Huong looked blank, disbelieving, her sombre eyes peculiarly oriental in their watchfulness.

'What do you mean, Miss Vandenburg?'

'Everybody's asking me that this evening. It's obvious, isn't it, that with those two in love and mooning around each other your career would mean nothing to Geoff any more? They'd want you to clear out and leave them alone.'

It was a very thoughtful Nurse Huong who finally made her way to the veranda where Benji-hadad was beginning to grow restless and roll his head fretfully in the sweat of his pillow.

Helen soon saw that the dinner, at least, was going to be a great success. As a cook Bahadur was inclined to the belief that if a dish was sufficiently highly seasoned it was edible and acceptable, but Ling John had obviously trained in a better school and had brought his cooking to a fine art.

The two ladies had dressed for the occasion and did credit to the men. Helen was in lavender, which complemented her grey eyes and gave them tones they did not normally possess. Like most of her clothes, the dress had to be washable, but it made up in dainty femininity what it lacked in material value, and draped in loving contours round her young bosom before frothing out at the waist. Her arms were perhaps a little too slim: Geoff found himself wondering how she had tackled that ghastly operation on Benji with such small—apparently inadequate—hands and forearms.

Celeste, in contrast, was in swathed brocade, a slinky,

slit-skirted orange-dragoned dress which had obviously been made in Hong Kong, so nearly did it favour the cheong-sam. The only concession from this national garb was that instead of its covering the chest entirely and ending in a small stand-up collar, nearly half of Celeste's natural womanly charms were exposed to the view of all, so that Edward wriggled occasionally and looked embarrassed.

The oysters having been served in chilled white wine, Ling John next sent in Bahadur with the curry. A fine breast of plump chicken was served to each lady, the legs to the gentlemen, then a wreathing of crackling rice, fried in melon-seed oil, which was really delicious. The curry sauce was suggestive of heat rather than hot, and there was a tray filled with tiny bowls of various garnishings, from ground-nuts to tinned orange rings.

'Your boy is a marvellous chef,' Helen addressed Geoff, for she could not get over the feeling that Edward was sulking a little. When she had told him there was to be a dinner party he had looked extremely reproachful and then said, 'Well! that cramps one's style somewhat, doesn't it? I would have thought as it's only one evening . . .' which was exactly what Helen had thought he might conclude.

'He's not so bad,' Geoff replied to her. 'He gets a bit lost for practice. You can borrow him any time you like.'

Edward laughed suddenly, smoothing his fair forelock back into place.

'That's good, McLeod! That's the way you get yourself invited to dinner, eh? You offer your cook's services.'

'I'm not quite with you, Courtenay . . .'

'Nobody's very bright this evening,' Celeste contributed. 'The doctor means you'd have nobody to cook *your* dinner and Helen would have to invite you here out of pity.'

'Helen's welcome to Ling John any time and can keep her pity into the bargain,' Geoff said sharply. 'Who's for more wine?'

Later on Celeste suddenly started the conversational ball rolling again.

'I've just really noticed that picture, Helen dear. It's of you, isn't it?'

They all gazed up at Howard Mitchell's mermaid with varying degrees of concentration.

'By jove, it *is* you, Helen!' Edward said somewhat offendedly. 'Of course, there was an artist bloke here before I went on leave. I say, isn't it a bit saucy, what?'

'What do you mean by "saucy"?' Helen asked.

'Did you pose for the artist?' Celeste wanted to know, showing friendly interest.

'He was always sketching,' Helen said innocently. 'Howard would suddenly say "Hold that!" whatever one was doing, and get busy with a pencil.'

'You can tell it's posed,' Celeste agreed, 'it's so absolutely *you*.' She sought Edward's eyes and he actually blushed. 'I suppose, living on an island alone with any one man, you do inevitably get to know one another awfully well.'

There was a feeling in the room as of lightning about to strike. But when something did strike it was more like the clean thrust of a dagger.

'Helen,' Geoff asked with a deadly intensity, 'did you pose in the *nude* for this fellow? That's what Celeste is itching to know.'

A blaze of scarlet rushed into Helen's pale cheeks immediately, so that as she indignantly repudiated the suggestion, she looked sparklingly beautiful, as a maiden always is in defence of her honour.

'Of course not. Howard and me—it wasn't like that. He painted this while I was on leave and left it for a present.'

'*You* seem to know Helen pretty well, McLeod,' observed Edward, still obviously rattled about something.

'One can know a person fundamentally in five minutes,' Geoff said crisply. 'The thing that struck me about her first was her youth. She's Primavera; eternal innocence and spring.'

'Will somebody pass me a bib?' asked Dr French, somewhat dejectedly, as she dug her spoon into a portion of cold melon.

CHAPTER THIRTEEN

'WELL, Helen,' Edward said tartly as he walked with her on the moonlit beach about an hour later, 'I can't say you seemed awfully keen to see me. Anybody would think we saw each other last week, or even last evening. I feel positively let down.'

'I'm sorry, Edward,' she said yet again. 'I really couldn't get out of this party tonight. Geoff McLeod seemed to think it would look odd if we dined in twos when there were only four of us to cater for. I saw his point at the time.'

'I don't dashed well see anything odd about splitting up. The brunette's his girl, isn't she?'

'I really don't know. She's not wearing any engagement ring.'

'Well, neither are you, but I still wanted to be alone with you. One doesn't have to advertise these things, does one?'

Helen's heart was beating painfully.

'Naturally I didn't presume you would want to be alone with me, Edward, when the arrangement was made about the dinner. I hadn't read your letter and it was the first word I'd had from you in more than three months. So much could have happened.'

He stopped in his tracks, leaned against the trunk of an areca palm and held out a hand to take hers.

'If you're truly sorry, I forgive you,' he said softly, and the handclasp became an urgent little tug of desire which sent her heart racing ahead of her thoughts. Keeping her head, however, she heard her voice saying, 'I'm not sure it's yours to forgive, Edward.'

The sudden blaze damped down immediately.

'What do you mean?' he asked, his face inscrutable in the shadows.

'I took some local leave when my contract finished. I—I heard you were—engaged.'

Her voice was almost a whisper. He dropped her hand while he thought fast.

'You heard this from a reliable source?'

'I would say two reliable sources. Dr Garland had read the announcement in *The Times*.'

'Confound it!' Helen was sure Edward blasted under his breath as he turned away and kicked up a small storm of silver sand.

She waited, her heart impatient, yet her head in full command, for his denial. It never came. Instead came a somewhat ungallant explanation and several excuses.

'Honestly, Helen, there was nothing at all to merit such an announcement, I can assure you. I had dinner with Morgath, the plastic surgeon, and met his daughter, Catherine. She was a bit on the dead keen side from the start, but one gets a bit lonely, you know? There was the odd spot of hugging and kissing after a few gins, nothing more than that . . .' Helen felt suddenly cold inside. 'I never spoke to her father or anything like that, or bought a ring, and next thing I knew I was being introduced as "my fiancé" and there was talk of a Christmas wedding. I told Cath she'd have to undo everything seeing that she'd taken things into her own hands, and there was a bit of a funeral tea, I can tell you, with Dad pointing out what a recant would do to his daughter socially, and hinting that I must have given her to understand I was serious for her to have done such a thing. Well—I mean,' she saw his shoulders hunch in a familiar shrug, 'one can't help one's natural charm, can one? I couldn't get away from London quickly enough, I can tell you. What an escape!'

He seemed to think the explanation sufficed and once more approached her, putting his hands on her shoulders.

'And now your periodic loneliness has seized you again, has it, Edward? If you make love to me I may be tempted to make an announcement myself. You can't keep on getting away with it.'

He stiffened, dropping his hands as though she was hot.

'What an unkind thing to say, Helen! I was the victim of circumstances, that's all. Cath wanted a husband.'

'So might I. Women do, you know. It's a normal biological urge with them. I once thought you wanted to marry me. I should hate to think you told another woman it was all of my doing.'

'Well, of course I wouldn't. And—in time, perhaps . . .' his resolution weakened and his voice wavered to a full stop. 'Helen,' he suddenly pleaded, 'what's up? Nothing's the same.'

'Of course it isn't,' she said coolly. 'You dropped me and forgot all about me while you immersed yourself in the excitement of a new affair. When there was a showdown you took the coward's way out and suddenly remembered little, understanding me, who kissed without telling and had no father in the offing to take a whip to you. Women aren't physically pleasurable pastimes, Edward. They begin to want more than kisses and promises. Their love has to know permanence or it won't grow and give and procreate. You are nobody's permanent lover. You want "kisses and cuddles" as you put it, but not at the expense of your freedom. I think I've grown up a lot in three months, and as far as I'm concerned we're friends and colleagues. Nothing more.'

There was a short, sharp silence during which her heart protested at the thought of her renouncement and the curling cream foam on the edge of the black silk water was like a backcloth to an unhappy scene in a play.

'It wouldn't be McLeod, would it?' Edward asked nastily. 'Maybe you want to cut in and put paid to the other girl's chances? They do say women are bitches when dealing with each other.'

'Evil speculations won't do *us* any good, Edward,' she said with admirable restraint. 'I think it was obvious at dinner that Geoff McLeod is not exactly mad about me. I'm Primavera, remember? Eternal youth, or something like that. I don't *have* to be in love with anybody, you know. Sometimes a rest from such things is as good as a holiday. Now I'm going back to the house. Are you coming for a last drink, or not?'

'No, thanks. I'll go to my hard little bed at the clinic and tell myself I've had two lucky escapes. Women are the very devil!'

He didn't offer to see her home. He strode off like a sulky little boy and took the cloud which had been over her spirits with him.

'I'm free of Edward,' she told herself firmly, 'and I think I'm glad. That poor girl in London—I hope *she* has the sense to be glad too!'

'Show me where you live, Geoffrey,' urged Celeste Vandenburg after dinner that same evening.

'Oh, all bungalows look alike on this island,' he replied easily. 'This is a much more comfortable place than mine.'

Celeste looked daggers at his handsome profile, and Dr Courtenay coughed uneasily.

'I think I'll have a look at the patient, if you'll excuse

me,' he said politely. 'I gather that's where our hostess has gone.'

Alone with her ex-fiancé at last, Celeste let fly.

'Need you make it so damned obvious, Geoffrey, that we're finished—through?' she half sobbed. 'I thought you loved me. My God!'

He watched her dispassionately, then rose and held out his hand.

'Come on, let's go for a walk,' he suggested, remembering how he had loved her once, and how her renouncement of him had stunned him, robbed him of all real feeling. He felt rather sad and yet relieved to realise that such metamorphosis had taken place in him that he was no longer capable of that love, but instead observed the object of his past delight with a stranger's eyes, which beheld her for what she really was, a scheming, disappointed, resentful and envious woman. She had hoped to break his will by ending their engagement; instead, she had lost him, and now she wanted him back on his terms; perhaps having realised that such a wonderful love would never be offered her again. She had openly admitted breaking her homeward journey halfway especially to see him. To this one brief reunion she had pinned all her hopes as a woman. Discarded, she would never hold her head quite so high again. Bitterness would seep into her very soul.

She had known others of her calling disappointed in love, and as she was almost twenty-nine she gave herself slender hopes of finding Geoff's equal in the marriage market should their break be final. The spinster nurse could look back on a hard training and an even harder future. Hospital life never became easier as one grew older and gained seniority. Eventually one gave up and took private work, one was bandied about, living in suitcases, attending funerals—for invariably the relatives had left it too late to do anything—and when one was older still one took night work, and became an old bat, knowing no social life at all and expected to be maid-of-all-work and human weight-lifter, just so long as the family weren't disturbed in their beds.

'After all, that's why we hired you, Nurse.'

Celeste blinked away this frightful picture of a blighted future and grabbed Geoff's arm.

'Are there snakes hereabouts?' she asked, trying to keep her tone light.

'Nothing dreadful,' he assured her, 'and I believe they sleep at night. Helen had a snake-bite case the other day. She gave the fellow a shot of serum and he was quite happy next day. Even without an injection, the worst they do is to put you to bed for four days or so.'

Celeste laughed tinklingly.

'Oh. Then I shall try to get bitten,' she told him, 'and then you'll have to keep me here.'

He said nothing, so she squeezed the arm she grasped and held it against her side, making him physically conscious of her in a way which nauseated him unaccountably.

'Would you mind?' she asked in a little-girl-lost voice.

He was still trying to sort out his feelings. Love had wreathed this creature beside him in an amazement of mystery: it had painted all her words with wisdom and her glances had been keys to the secrets of all earthly delights she kept within her soft, feminine body and her bright, challenging mind.

What had happened to change her?

He had watched her at dinner, shocked by the mask of pretence that couldn't hide the malice in her eyes when she engaged Helen in what appeared on the surface to be a casual conversation.

He was sorry for her, but he could feel nothing more.

To force his lips to kiss her in consolation would be a falsehood. He had no kisses left to give her.

'You would mind, wouldn't you?' she insisted sighingly. 'I don't think you even like me any more.'

'Celeste,' he said with some asperity, 'there's no question of my liking you or not. I was in love with you and we were engaged for nearly four years. That's a deuced long time, but I worshipped you nearly every minute of it. When I was given the chance of doing this research I wanted to hasten our marriage so we could get away together. I seem to remember that what followed was none of my doing. The way you carried on at times I was led into wondering if you had ever loved me. I kept pleading with you, I was even on my knees at your feet when you slung that ring in my face and told me exactly what I could do with both my "miserable bauble" and myself. I didn't accept my dismissal lightly, Celeste, and you'll never know what I went through while I was waiting for the plane that last week, hoping and expecting you'd turn up and say you were sorry.'

'It was a question of choosing between your new job and me,' she said thinly.

'Not to me. It seemed I should have my opportunities for advancement *and* my wife, in that order. No woman should hold a man's career in her hands.'

'Our dear lords and masters,' she sneered.

'Rubbish! A man is either a leaning post or a leaner. I never intend to be the latter.'

'Such a big, strong man!' she sneered again.

He paused, utterly sickened by now.

'May I take you back now to the bungalow?'

'Of course. We can be one big happy family again, have an exciting game of whist, or something.'

But when they returned there was only Nurse Huong

to greet them. She told them that the two doctors had gone for a walk.

'It must be something in the air,' commented Celeste. 'I hope Primavera's having a better time than I did. You may go,' she told Geoff acidly. 'Blossom and I can occupy an hour well enough without the pleasure of your company.'

He turned, feeling enraged all of a sudden.

'Do I need to come down in the morning?' he asked coldly, as Nurse Huong disappeared quickly in case there should be goodbyes to be said between these two.

'No. Don't bother. As far as I'm concerned you're dead and buried, Geoff McLeod.'

He looked at her, but still restrained himself.

'Goodnight, then,' he said, and the sound of her sobs exploding all around followed him like curses as he hastened away into the shadow of the trees.

CHAPTER FOURTEEN

A NIGGLE of regret for what was now so irretrievably past troubled Helen briefly next morning, as she watched the launch leave for the last time, carrying Edward, alone, sitting rather stiffly and starchily in the stern. He showed at his best professionally, and he had been so very gentle, so concerned over Benji-hadad, who had succumbed to tears at the finish, not over his pains as he was jolted about, but in the prospect of leaving his family so precipitately.

Here the man Karim, who was also on his way to hospital, had been a help.

'Me too. Both together,' he had comforted the lad. 'We come back very important men. Have much to tell.'

Benji pondered on this, saw his sister weeping into their mother's sarong and decided on a better show. Tears were for children and women, not for very important men.

While waiting for the launch's return, Edward had said casually:

'I may not come next trip, Helen, but someone will be along, of course.'

'Of course,' she agreed, flushing a little. 'I hope you'll see I get reports of the progress of those two in hospital, so I can keep their families posted.'

'I'll see you do.' He held out his hand, still pale from his leave. 'Goodbye for now, Helen.'

'Goodbye, Edward.'

'I'm sorry you think I'm the love 'em and leave 'em type.'

'You won't be,' she told him, 'when you meet the right girl.'

But she knew that Edward would never meet the 'right' girl. If he married it would have to be for a very good reason, and being in love wasn't a good enough reason for someone like him.

She continued watching the narrow opening into the bay until two hoots from the invisible *Madrassi Belle* told her she was leaving Fan-Cho waters.

It would be a whole month, a little eternity, until the vessel called again.

All at once the island seemed a lonely, infinitesimal dot in a vast, empty ocean, and seeing the long stretch of silver sand, now empty of people, Helen was conscious of the swift panic of desire to undo the past twenty-four hours and still be able to lay claim to someone who was at least fond of her—if only in a dallying way—rather than accept the loneliness the scene conjured up, reflecting the desert that was her life.

She caught herself up sharply, shook herself, closed her eyes and talked to herself like a dutch uncle.

'The trouble with you, my girl, is that you have too little to occupy you. You enjoyed having all that to do for young Benji and it's his going you're regretting, really, but for selfish reasons. Get your books out. Catch up with your reading. Keep yourself occupied . . .'

'I'm fond of doing crosswords myself,' came an unexpected, lazy masculine voice into her soliloquy. 'What's all this, Helen? Self-analysis?'

She flushed readily and smiled up at her questioner. She was surprised to find she was genuinely pleased to see Geoff McLeod.

'I often talk to myself,' she laughed, trying to remember exactly what it was she had said. 'They say it comes of being too much alone, don't they? Do you think I'm far gone?'

'I think you'll pass here on Fan-Cho,' he said in the same light tones, 'but if you start that lark in Leicester Square they'll put you away in no time!'

He had turned with her as though to accompany her back to her house.

'You didn't come down before when they were leaving, did you?' she suddenly reflected. Celeste Vandenburg had seemed in a particularly foul temper, she remembered, especially when she snatched her make-up case from a youth who was carrying it and it had fallen into the surf, the yellow foam seeping in among the various bottles and jars. 'We got everybody away all right,' she added quickly.

'No, I didn't come down. I hate goodbyes. I said mine to Celeste last evening.'

Helen wondered how tender their goodbye had been. Personally she wasn't sorry to have her house to herself again.

'I thought I might invite myself to lunch,' Geoff went on, in some embarrassment. 'Your house is handy and I want to talk to you.'

'Oh!' Helen was frankly startled. She had played hostess last evening, put on a fine show and now frankly didn't know what remained in the fridge. 'I usually only have a chapatti—Bahadur bakes them—and a cup of coffee. Why not come to dinner? He'll be putting something better than that on for dinner.'

A muscle twitched at the corner of Geoff's mouth.

'No,' he said very firmly. 'I particularly want to talk to you now, in daylight. Food doesn't matter.'

Helen relented immediately.

'We'll share what there is. Chapattis, tomatoes and—

fresh pineapple. I didn't mean to imply you weren't welcome.'

Bahadur, determined that no Chinese was going to outshine him a second time, opened a tin of tongue and served it on the best willow pattern plates with a large bowl of salad swimming in dressing.

'He doesn't give one the option,' Helen explained as they sat down on the shady side of the veranda, 'and as he puts curry and mustard into everything, one needs lettuce to cool one's tongue.'

The meal was nearly over and the conversation had been light and pleasant, but Helen knew there was a real reason behind the meeting that hadn't yet been disclosed.

'You wanted to speak to me seriously, didn't you, Geoff? I'm all ears whenever you're ready.'

She poured coffee, feeling his embarrassment as a tangible thing.

'Yes. It's difficult. Last night Celeste—and Courtenay—gave me to understand our position here is somewhat odd. Actually I don't agree, but it was pointed out to me that certain people ashore may hear about us and presume the worst. They're the ones with cesspool minds, of course. It's what you think that counts with me, Helen, and I want you to be absolutely frank with me. You were put to it explaining your relationship with the artist fellow who was here, and I don't want you to be driven into explaining us. Why should you be subjected to embarrassments simply because unattached males decide to invade your little kingdom? I suppose the artist was a free-lance type who could park anywhere he fancied, but I'm under a department, and, though they knew there was a doctor in residence here, they didn't seem to know your sex. You were a surprise to me, I can tell you. Perhaps if they knew they'd want to dis-attach me and send me elsewhere. Lots of couples just couldn't survive our situation without succumbing either to—er—romance, or something less acceptable to polite society. But we know ourselves, don't we, Helen? Nothing like that troubles you and me?'

She was staring at him blankly, so that he thought her somewhat obtuse. Surely he had already made his point very clear?

'If you're remembering that time when I kissed you—when you had been drinking—' he reminded her, 'I only did it out of sheer cussedness. I didn't want you making a habit of your visits and it was a sure way of driving you away—that is if you were a nice girl.'

Her eyes were now not only even more round, but blazing.

'I—I just don't know to which statement I should take exception first,' she exploded. 'Of all the ungallant speeches from a man to any woman, I should think that just about takes the cake! But I shan't itemise. I shall simply tell you I understand perfectly what you're getting at, so you needn't try to translate it into words of one syllable. What you're trying to say is that you and I would be safe from one another's attentions on an island six foot by three, if required, let alone on the Isles of Nowhere. I agree with you, absolutely, but this is true only because *I* have decided that it should be so. I find you egotistical, aggressive, unimaginative and unattractive. I wouldn't even glance your way in a crowd. Here I do have to see you occasionally, but it's not from choice. You're someone moving in the background, neither desired nor regretted; mostly not even noticed. I hope *I* make myself quite clear too?'

Geoff looked slightly put out.

'Well, there's no need to harangue about it. I simply

want to know that it will neither inconvenience nor embarrass you if I finish my research on Fan-Cho.'

Helen actually managed a light laugh, like ice cubes tinkling on glass.

'No more than a column of ants crossing my compound. Finish your research by all means.'

'Did Courtenay seem to think I should leave?'

'He didn't say so. Edward Courtenay happens to be another entirely affected by his own importance.'

'I thought he was rather keen on you. So did Celeste.'

'I hope you can bear to be wrong on occasions.'

'If you're going to stay upon your ridiculous high horse, I'm going.'

'Do. Whenever you like.'

'I suppose I should have said you were sweet and lovely, that I couldn't keep away from you; flattered your vanity with insincerity.'

Helen smoothed her eyebrows with a flick.

'*My* reactions would have remained the same, Mr McLeod, but I might have wondered whom you were deceiving; myself or Miss Vandenburg.'

'If you really want to know, Celeste and I have said goodbye for ever.'

'Oh, I'm sorry!' Helen said in genuine regret, then bounced back into her assumed rôle once more. 'I should be careful, though, if I were you. Men do queer things on the rebound. Even if you do make overtures to me I shall be on my guard, knowing you're sick emotionally.'

'Emotional poppycock!' he said sharply, rising to leave at last. 'I thought a few days ago what a dam' good little doctor you were, the way you tackled that boy and got him patched up. I thought there was something remarkable about you. But now I know you're just as idiotic as the rest of 'em where your feminine pride's concerned. You *want* me to fall for your charms, deny it as you will.'

'I—I—' stammered Helen furiously.

Geoff's finger wagged from the bottom of the veranda steps.

'I know you better now, and so I beware of all your claims that you're self-sufficient; a snow-maiden locked in a lonely, high tower. They're the sort who use all their ingenuity to drop a rope to the errant knight. Think over what I've said, Dr French. Think it over.'

And Helen, wishing she had a six-shooter in her hand filled with small, stinging darts, watched the broad, immaculately shirted back disappearing from her ken.

CHAPTER FIFTEEN

THE young man with the smooth, pale coffee-coloured skin of his kind emerged from the wind-swept shrub of the higher rain forest and began to follow the track leading up the rocky slopes which formed the conical centre of the main island of Fan-Cho. He paused a moment, about a thousand feet up, to wonder at the view, which never ceased to excite him, though he came here but rarely, being nervous of the spirits said to exist up here.

Daylight was more reassuring, however, than when these tales of the supernatural were told in the evening round the fires, and he thrilled as he saw the islet of Ay-oh now completely in his ken, and not more than four hundred feet at its highest point. Two other islets, only partially seen from this vantage point, were hardly more than pancakes, so flat where they, and when the monsoon arrived with its winds and rain-storms, the islanders quickly took off in their catamarans to visit their relations who were geographically placed to withstand the tidal waves of more than twenty feet in height which sometimes washed over these otherwise paradisaic places.

The youth decided to squat and eat his lunch, though the sun was still more than two hours from its zenith. From a fold of cloth around his waist he took two round, flat cakes made from pounded maize. Between them he placed a fish, smoked, stinking, species unknown. He thought it a very tasty morsel indeed, however, and ate it up, bones and all.

After a belch or two of sheer enjoyment, he was ready for his slice of coconut, but this dried his mouth, so he fished behind his neck and brought a bottle into view, an item which looked sharply incongruous in the general picture of a being who might have been Adam himself, alone in Creation. The bottle was made of plastic and had a red stopper. The youth could just as well have drunk from a hollow tube of bamboo, but he had purchased the bottle from Simbat-lal and paid for it with several fine pieces of mother-of-pearl. It was now one of his most treasured possessions and he had cuffed a small brother severely only that morning for daring to touch it.

He climbed again, up and up, watchful for the snakes and scorpions which favoured the rocks warmed by the sun. Up and up, he went, panting and sweating, now harried by the rough, hot wind which held no refreshment in its breath.

Finally he came to the dark yawn of a cave, and paused uncertainly, his heart pounding, This was always the moment when just anything might happen, he had been taught to fear. He had come to call Old Brother from his lair to accompany him down the track to witness the marriage of his sister Va-tu and Kali, son of Simbat-lal, the trader, but the old ones had told him that Old Brother was not really a holy man at all, but a demon, and could change his shape at will. If a serpent came to the cave entrance, or a bear, then he was to turn and run, shrieking loudly, and everybody would hasten, armed with sticks, to rescue him.

But after only a moment of uncertainty an old man, much scarred from shaving with rusty knives and the like, appeared in the cave entrance. His face was wrinkled, like parchment, and his expression remote and kind. He wore the saffron-coloured robe of the Buddhists, and had lived in this cave for more years than the youth could remember, so that the robe was now tattered and scarcely hid the old man's wasted limbs.

The lad gave his message in a trembling voice. There was a marriage. Would Old Brother descend to the village and bless the union?

The priest bowed in acquiescence and disappeared for a moment. He was always called to witness at marriages and deaths, though otherwise he never interfered in the islanders' affairs. Like an eagle in its eyrie, he spent his life above the small petty doings of the human race as a whole. He lived as close to God as he knew how, yet never rejected a plea to share his inner knowledge with others when it was asked or required of him. Now he appeared carrying a staff and his enamel begging bowl. He never moved without them.

The drums, which had started the day with the first cock-crow, persisted without abatement by the hour. Helen had been to other weddings, and now recognised the wedding rhythm. The island was soon covered in a pall of woodsmoke, for so many visitors were expected from the other islands there was much cooking to be done.

There was no point in holding a surgery, of course, for all, even those not in the best of health, would be attending the wedding and keeping all their physical troubles for tomorrow or the next day. The bismuth bottle and plenty of laxatives had better be in the foreground after all the feasting that a marriage ceremony entailed.

Noon was the time set for the business side of things, then there was all afternoon for eating and drinking and all evening for dancing and merrymaking and drinking again.

Helen hoped the one baby expected at any moment by a member of her flock would have the decency to allow his mother to enjoy herself, in as much peace as nature allows women in such a condition, until after the celebrations. The child was already two days overdue according to her reckoning, and these people kept pretty well to the calendar in these matters.

Because of the heat she dressed coolly in fine lemon cotton, a dress she had acquired during her recent leave, and did her hair in plaits which she then wound round her head. A large-brimmed straw hat completed the picture. Suddenly a figure appeared outside on the veranda.

'Oh!' she cried out in surprise. 'Just a minute!'

She had time to harden her heart before sailing in to confront Geoff McLeod in the living-room.

'Yes?' she enquired, with some asperity.

Surprise had been met with surprise, however. Her appearance not only surprised but stunned him. He had never seen anything so dainty, sweet or cool-looking since he last saw a daffodil in an English garden.

'You look smashing!' he said in honest approval.

Helen naturally felt flattered first, then uncertain and suspicious afterwards.

'Here!' she warned him. 'None of that! Beware the Greeks when they bring gifts . . .'

'I know.' He too was dressed up for the occasion in a white suit with a striped tie lying against his fresh-looking shirt. 'You must have a mighty poor opinion of me. I don't blame you. I suppose I really asked for that tirade I brought on the other day.'

'Which tirade?' Helen asked, liking to think of herself as always calm and in full command of her temper. 'I'm sure there's no need for you to apologise. I'm quite happy with things left as they were between us.'

'Well, I'm not,' he said fiercely. 'I came here to try and explain and you're not going to stop me.'

'If you're going to be all masculine and dictatorial . . .' she said offhandedly.

'I am. Sit down!' he told her, and much to her amazement she sat down, half expecting him to use force if she refused.

'Now get one thing straight, Helen French,' he said without more ado, 'I don't intend to carry on a schoolkid tiff with you while we're both here on Fan-Cho. You can cut out the la-di-dah and the hoy-foloy stuff as from now.'

'Well!' she gasped.

'. . . And kindly have the goodness to shut up for five minutes. I'll take you to the "do" in good time. The other day I was gauche with you. I said everything I had to say in the worst possible way. At the time I couldn't understand why you blew up, but later on, when I thought about what I'd said, I tried to put myself in your shoes and I—I think you were right to explode. I suppose, with all due modesty, I'm good at my job, but I've had nothing to do with women as a whole. After I met Celeste there wasn't anyone else, you see.

'That's why I *must* explain what I meant the other day. It was you I was thinking of, your reputation and feelings. You might have had a young man somewhere who would have gone potty at the idea of me roaming around here: even the best-intentioned of young men get jealous very easily when a girl's pretty enough. And—and that's what I meant to say, that you—no one—need be worried by the thought of my presence on the island. I—I wouldn't take advantage of you or—or anything. It's such a damned difficult thing to put into words, you see, and I realised afterwards it may have seemed as though I was saying you weren't attractive.'

They both looked rather miserably down at their hands.

'Which wouldn't be at all true,' he went on quietly and sincerely. 'You're very sweet and attractive, Helen, and I can see many fellows telling you so, given half a chance, but I'm rather bewildered and—and numb, if you see what I mean. . . ?'

She looked up.

'You mean about everything being over between you and Celeste?'

'Yes,' he looked away again. 'It went on a long time. I can't realise . . .'

She sighed sympathetically and patted his hand.

'I do understand, I think. I'm a bit numb myself. I'm getting over someone too.'

'Courtenay?' he demanded.

She flushed.

'Well—yes, if you must know.'

'I thought he was inclined to put the brand mark on you. The lingering glance, the inflexion in the voice, etcetera.'

'Well, it's off now,' she said shortly.

'Good! I mean—well—I can't see him and you, some-how.'

'Whom *can* you see—and me?' she asked with sarcastic interest.

'Oh,' he pondered, 'he must have a bigger heart than Courtenay, and I think he'll turn up eventually.'

'On Fan-Cho?'

'Hardly on Fan-Cho, unless he's washed up from a shipwreck, heaven forbid!'

'Exactly!' she informed him. 'When I finish my latest contract I shall be an elderly lady of almost twenty-eight, and girls mature very early back home, you know. In view of the competition I can foretell my own future,

thank you. I shall retire into general practice and count
time's passing by the epidemics I survive, *not* the patter-
ing of my grandchildren's little feet!'

He was regarding her with one eyebrow raised in
disbelief.

'You don't mean to tell me you're a day over twenty-
two at this moment?'

She laughed this to scorn, liking it nevertheless.

'How long do you think it takes a doctor to qualify?
Even though I went into medicine straight from school it
still took full five and a half years out of my young life.
I've been here three and a half years. Where's your
arithmetic?'

He blinked his eyes.

'You still don't look a day over twenty-two,' he insisted. 'But I suppose I must treat you with greater
respect from here on.'

'Yes, do that,' she smiled up at him. 'Now I think we'd
better go to the wedding.'

'But as friends?' he asked her, holding out his big
brown hand.

'Of course. Friends,' she agreed, putting her hand into
his.

'Good!' He savoured the idea and apparently liked it,
tucking her arm through his and drawing her out on to
the veranda. 'Why do people have to spoil everything by
falling in love?' he asked darkly. 'I think being friends is
a happier state, don't you?'

She looked at him shyly from under her yellow-
brimmed hat.

'I think as we're going to a wedding, Geoff, we simply
have to believe in love on a general principle. But you
and I can be happy as friends. Let's leave it like that,
shall we?'

'Now I know why you're so wise at times,' he pondered, 'it's because of your real age. I couldn't understand such a young-looking kid being so wise.'

In case he had said the wrong thing again, he squeezed her arm and smiled at her most reassuringly.

CHAPTER SIXTEEN

'WHO's the bloke in the orange nightie?' Geoff asked in the languorous heat of the afternoon, enjoying yet again the way his companion went into silent ripples under the yellow cotton of her dress before her laughter found tongue. 'I haven't seen him before, have I?'

'You really mustn't, Geoff,' she told him with a quick straightening of her features. 'Klandok is a holy man. He's rather touched in the head, I think, but he gives an air of respectability to these occasions. He drinks, unfortunately, and is inclined to run around stark naked after a time, but he never harms anyone, and after he has slept it off he dons his rags and goes back to his meditations. Which reminds me, I really must get him a length of material for a new robe. I'll get it sent out on the next boat and take it up to him. The exercise will do me good.'

'You mean you'll climb the hill?'

'Why not? I've got legs, haven't I?'

'You've got very nice legs,' he said in a swift appreciation, 'But what about sending your menfolk on such errands? There are more snakes up there than I care to think about. We can't have our doctor getting bitten.'

She rather liked that 'our doctor' bit, and dwelt on it a moment.

'Bahadur, my bearer, will do anything on earth for me but go near a heathen,' she smiled. 'Pagans he excuses, but not heathen. As his Memsahib he accepts me, but he often tries to convert me. I think he would have made a marvellous missionary if he hadn't lost his power of speech.'

'Then what about your orderly?'

'Vikrit? Oh—he's very rigid about where his duties begin and end. He's a frustrated doctor, you know, and I think he tells the islanders *he* employs *me*! Going errands up mountains wouldn't suit "Dr" Vikrit, at all!'

'Then when you get the new robe *I'll* go up with it, or—better still—we'll both go. I think friends occasionally take a stroll? Don't they?'

She looked at him from under surprisingly long, golden-brown eyelashes. He hadn't noticed how they curled before.

'Very well,' she agreed, rather glad that an interruption was forthcoming in the form of a young girl bearing a basket of sliced melon wrapped in palm-leaves. 'As good as a drink,' she murmured, as the half-sweet juice cooled her mouth.

The occasion was so far proving very pleasant, she pondered contentedly. Geoff McLeod was a good, amusing companion and had kept her entertained without ever becoming malicious in his humour. Occasionally he left her and took a few hundred feet of film with his fine ciné camera, having been given the necessary permission to do so by the headman and the island council. They knew what film was, having been film actors before for the American company which had called on them.

Thus he had wonderful shots of the bridal ceremony, with Va-tu (whose French-sounding name really meant the 'plump one') being dragged reluctantly to meet her bridegroom and being forced to kiss each of his feet in turn. After this act of submission it was Kali's prerogative either to accept or decline his bride by offering—or withholding—his hand. Kali had decided to accept, and after the two had eaten and drunk, the girl suddenly gave a wild shriek and darted off into the shadow of tamarinds circling the clearing. Kali had immediately dashed after her, accepting a thonged raffia rope from his father's hand with which to whip his bride into quick submission once again.

Ignoring this decidedly pagan ritual, however, the figure of Klantok, in his saffron tatters, had called down the blessing of God upon the event. He wailed loudly and long in an unknown tongue, and then prostrated himself, face down, under a tree. Food and arrack were placed beside him and he was then ignored, allowed to recover and refresh himself at will.

'When are the happy couple rejoining their guests?' Geoff now asked, as Va-tu's voice could be heard shrieking abuse in the distance.

'Oh, they don't,' Helen shrugged. 'They stay out there together all the rest of the day and night. In the morning Va-tu decides whether or not she likes being married to Kali. If she doesn't they call the whole thing off. If she does, however, they go happily off to Ba-ba island—the uninhabited one—for their honeymoon. Kali's been busy for weeks building a hut there. They'll just about get a week or so in before the monsoon drives them back.'

'Supposing Kali decides he doesn't want to go on being married to *her*?'

'Oh, he's had his chance. It's up to him to—to make her like him tonight.'

'So he's gone about it with a whip?'

'Oh,' she shrugged, 'that used to worry me, but it's only part of the show. Here men are supposed to be the dominant sex and the women love it. Actually Va-tu won't come to any harm or have any bruises to show. Kali will crack his whip and she will make a great deal of noise, but it will only be for our benefit.'

'Do you think they'll stay married?'

'I think Kali is the likeliest lad for her on the islands. I have known, when there were three unattached youths hanging around, a girl who *did* change her mind after her wedding night. She tried again with number two after three months, but it was number one's daughter I delivered in due season. This gave two a chance to separate from her, which he did, and she finally married number three and they're very happy with two sons and the original daughter. They're good parents, fortunately.'

'You make it all sound very simple and have a surprising knowledge of these people. If I can sell my film, will you write the commentary?'

'I suppose I could try. I've often thought of writing a book, but there are always my studies to contend with. I may eventually write my book when I have both my membership and—perhaps—a fellowship.'

'I suppose when that day dawns you'll pass a mere dentist by as being beneath your contempt?'

'You're no mere dentist, Geoff, as you very well know. But if you were, I'd still acknowledge you, complete with my FRCP.'

'Big of you,' he smiled lazily, and lay down full length so that he saw her face from below, pale and clear-complexioned, with a dimple in each cheek when she smiled. 'How's the tooth?' he asked.

'Please don't remind me of that episode,' she begged, with a shudder. 'I never knew they could make one so miserable. Why did you take up dentistry?'

'Oh, I don't really know. It wasn't with any noble idea of serving mankind, I can tell you. I suppose I was really steered into it by my parents. My mother wanted me to be a doctor, my father—who was stockbreeding by that time, having retired from the Foreign Service—wanted a veterinary surgeon in the family, so while I was thinking about my future I got down to studying anatomy for a start. We had polo ponies (a non-paying pastime); a dairy herd (definitely a paying proposition) and a small flock of Suffolk sheep. I practised my anatomy on the animals. It was merely incidental that I found their teeth interesting; you know, each type equipped for their job as either tearers or choppers or chewers. I began to think about human teeth and learned we have just about the lot, tearers *and* choppers *and* chewers. I was horrified to realise most people don't use half their teeth for the proper purpose, and that fifty per cent of twelve-year-old children back home have decaying permanent teeth! Did *you* know that? Well—one thing led to another, and here I am, quite happy in my job.'

'Research going all right?'

'Fine, thanks. If some of the muck they've served for this feast is accountable for the lack of decay in the Fan-Choans, generally, I'm all for upper and lower plates next week!'

Again Helen rippled into laughter.

'Oh, Geoff, you *are* a fool! I never laughed so much in years.'

He looked up at her very seriously for a moment.

'Then the friendship is a success, is it?'

She sighed, wishing he wouldn't rub in their relationship so often and relentlessly.

'It's a success,' she agreed, and lay down beside him on the colourful carpet which had been allotted them, putting her shady hat over her eyes and looking up through its lacery at the blue of the sky which was somehow metallic today and hard.

A masculine arm shifted and touched hers briefly. An electric communion—which she hoped was obvious only to her—was the result.

She lay puzzling things out, wondering why such

reflexes were none of love. If she was alone with Geoff, and turned on her side towards him, he would probably prove flint to her tinder and they would burn together in the consuming flame they had created for their pleasure.

But it wouldn't be love.

It was all so utterly disconcerting knowing there were such inflammable ingredients on Fan-Cho, and no matches!

Her lips smiled at her metaphor, below the hat brim, and Geoff, watchful, saw this and reached for her hand to squeeze it gently. He found instead the fingers locked his as in a vice, and when he looked again she was smiling no more. Her lips, he saw, were parted slightly and rather tense. He whipped away her hat and gazed into startled eyes, and in his chest a hammer knocked with responsive urgency.

'Look! Klantok's off again!' she cried, to distract him, as the old hermit scratched at his face and poured sandy dust over his head.

The moment of danger passed, unacknowledged, between them, and for the rest of the day they wisely kept their friendship flourishing without the stimulus of physical contact.

CHAPTER SEVENTEEN

THE sky turned to violet, deep purple and then black; not a leaf stirred on the trees and the sea looked like oil, only broken into a white curl where the reef had formed, a natural barrier to keep strangers and their ships away.

It was oppressive in a way that was almost tangible; the heavy air lay like a load upon one's head and shoulders. A parrot squawked idly and was still, waiting under what natural cover there was for the storm to break.

When it did it was as though everything happened at once. White lightning rent the curtain of the sky and let the deluging waters through: the rain fell like a waterfall, almost as deafening as the thunder which rocked the island. In less than five minutes there were lakes where the compounds had been and a streaming from roofs and treetops. Two trees were washed completely from their rootings and deposited more than five yards away, doomed to die and rot there where they lay.

In half an hour it was over, the clouds rolled southwest in the direction of Sri Lanka and the sun broke over Fan-Cho, smiling, gobbling up the stream and turning to limp humidity what had become a tedium of heat.

Helen emerged from the bungalow with Bahadur to survey the wreckage of the first assault of the season, if any. The compound lake had already disappeared, but it was a novelty to walk on soft earth: there was actually mud on her shoes as she shaded her eyes against the glare of the sun and surveyed the roof.

120

'You seem to have made a good job of it,' she told the bearer. 'It still appears to be in one piece.'

His speaking fingers replied that there was more—much more—to come.

'Yes, I know. Much as I hate to say this, you'd better fix the shutters at the windows before you leave this evening.'

She stayed on in the compound after he had left her to take in the moist, scented air. Every growing thing exuded a fragrance, whether it be sweet or spicy, after rain. Tomorrow—or the next day—there would be new grass and carpets of exotic flowers, whose life was but a day, yet whose sweetness was unsurpassed. There would be violets as big as pansies and gaudy anemones of every hue. Though it was October, Helen thought of this season as spring, and when the flowering trees and shrubs burgeoned, which would be soon, the whole island was like an enchanted garden and fairies could surely not be far away.

'Hello!' called Geoff McLeod cheerfully.

'Hello!' Helen returned. 'What brings you at this hour?'

'Well, actually, I wondered if you were house-whole, to coin a word. I've lost part of my veranda.'

'Perhaps I should have warned you. We get heavy weather here when the monsoon does start. You had better round up some of the villagers to build you up and batten your roof down before another storm comes our way.'

'I've already done that. Fortunately I had half a dozen of my dental guinea-pigs on the spot and I've left them busily at it. Some weatherwise soul among them had decided today was not a day to be caught out at sea. You're all right, then?'

'Yes, thanks. Bahadur's gone to look out the shutters.

It will be hot in bed tonight with the windows sealed up. Can you spare the time for a cup of tea?'

'I was hoping you'd suggest just that. Actually I'm well forward with my work. I told Blossom that I was leaving her to see to things and taking an hour or so off to come and talk to you. That is if you're not busy?'

'Actually I was trying to concentrate on the fascinating subject of albinism in mammals. I wasn't getting far. Waiting for a storm to break makes one too tense for study, doesn't it?'

She had not meant her observation to sound ambiguous, but Geoff's direct glance made her colour rise immediately, and the playful twitching of his lips told her he had observed.

'What do you want to see me about?' she asked, as she poured the tea.

'Nothing,' he said blankly. 'Should I have a reason for coming to chat with my friend?'

'No,' she said, this time controlling her blushes. These were not the prerogative of a man's 'friends', she decided wryly. 'I just thought maybe there was something special. You said your work was well in hand?'

'Yes. Actually it begins to run parallel with yours from now on.'

'How do you mean?'

'I've reached a point where I would like to check the medical records of some people against my findings. There is calcium deficiency in only two of my "patients". Naturally I would like to know if they have been yours at any time, and for what reason.'

'All my files are kept at the clinic,' said Helen. 'Would you care to . . . ?'

'No, thank you. There's no hurry. It'll do any time. It's close, isn't it?'

'Undo your tie,' she invited, pouring him a second cup of tea.

'Now you should know better than ask me to do that,' he chided her. 'I would feel half dressed without my tie.'

'But surely you relax sometimes?' she demanded. 'Don't tell me you go to bed in one?'

'Are you trying to be provocative again?' he asked quietly, seizing one of her wrists in a band of steel and forcing her to keep still while he brought his face close to hers. 'I do *not* sleep in a tie, young lady, and neither do I expect to go to bed in this house. Therefore I have no excuse for removing what I consider to be a necessary accessory to a gentleman's attire.'

She began to struggle playfully, but didn't make much headway.

'I shouldn't like you to be really mad at me,' she gasped breathlessly. 'I need that arm, if you don't mind, Geoff.'

'Do you?' he released it slowly, ruefully rubbing where the circulation had been temporarily strangulated. 'There's not much of you, is there, Helen? You must have been a tiny baby.'

'On the contrary, they called me "Dimples" for the first five years of my life. I was quite a podgy schoolgirl too. Fan-Cho has slimmed me down considerably.'

'You mean you had curves and things?' he asked disbelievingly.

She looked down at herself.

'What am I supposed to have now? Angles?'

When she looked up at him again they both laughed spontaneously, enjoying their laughter until it was spent.

'You're all right, Helen,' he assured her. 'Some would say if there was more to you the merrier; but I think you're a good little half pint in the right size bottle.'

'That must surely rank as the most unusual compliment paid on these shores, at least.'

'I'm an unusual fellow.'

'So I have gathered.'

They laughed again, and Bahadur, reaching their part of the veranda from the back of the house, smiled with a flash of white teeth as he heard them. Memsahib Doctor laughed little enough, and it was good that someone was making her happy like this.

The bearer gained attention and delivered his message, sad that the laughter should change so quickly to dismay.

'Oh, no!' Helen said sharply.

'What's he say?' Geoff demanded, not understanding the sign language.

'It's Mahele, my mother-to-be. Her child is now almost two weeks overdue, and because she has grown impatient with the waiting time she has gone back home to Ay-oh. She was staying on Fan-Cho with her married sister so that I could keep an eye on her. Now that she's back home she's in labour—difficult labour. All this came over on the drums.'

Geoff tried to interpret the needs of the moment from the story.

'So do they bring her to you, or do you go to her?'

'I must go.'

'It's going to storm again at any moment, you know.'

'Yes, I do know. I must hurry!'

'I'll take you in my boat.'

'No. There's Vikrit . . .'

'I'd rather you were in my charge in a storm than in his.'

'Very well. Fortunately my bag's packed for this very emergency, though I hadn't counted on taking it to sea. Come on!'

They ran through the palms and tamarinds down to the beach and Geoff wrenched the tarpaulin cover from his motor-boat.

'She's heavier than yours and will ride better. Let's hope we get through the gap in the reef before hell is let loose again.'

The sky was purple-black to the north-east and rapidly blotting out the steel-blue which remained. Thunder rumbled distantly, and against the dark curtain the lightning made a constant electrical display, throwing stark patterns in sharp outlines as though a master hand held a finger nervously on the heavenly main switch.

Helen refused to think of what might happen, if——

When the first rain drops fell with the first thunder-flash she looked ahead towards Ay-oh, now blotted out by the curtain of the rain. They had both donned oilskins as they embarked, but even so the weight of water descending, and that shipped, was soon considerable.

'Bale, dear!' Geoff's voice roared from the stern.

Helen crept into the well of the boat and busied herself with the can she had found under one of the seats. She had been working for five minutes or more before she realised he had called her 'dear' so naturally.

The sea was now like ink all around them, white-crested ink, with each crest trying to break in the boat for Helen to feverishly bale out again. It was a man and woman alone against the might of elements more terrible than ever atomic energy has conceived, and yet Helen worked with an assured confidence—in the midst of great physical discomfort—never doubting they would reach their objective in due time.

The purple canopy had passed over, and the westering sun shone gaudily as they eventually beached on the battered shore of Ay-oh, the second largest island in the group.

'Thanks,' Helen said briefly, squelching her way up the beach. 'I'll be—you know where?'

'I'll find you,' said Geoff, beaching the boat.

Helen's presence was greeted with a wildness of grief she had not expected as she reached Mahele's house. Nobody had realised she would come, owing to the storm. None of the menfolk had stirred on the treacherous waters all day. They clustered, hangdog, in a nearby house. In the house of birth the attendant women moaned and wept.

'What's wrong?' Helen asked in her no-nonsense voice, as she approached Mahele lying immobile on her palliasse bed. She could see the birth was over.

An old woman, who was not the best recommended of Fan-Cho's midwives, came forward and announced the child, a boy, had been stillborn after a long and difficult birth.

Helen's heart sank to her shoes.

'Oh, no!' she cried out, then looked at the old woman anew.

'Where is the child?' she feverishly demanded.

'Is dead, Min Hana. Nothing to be done.'

'I want the child brought to me. At once.'

The old woman looked annoyed for a moment, then shrugged and turned away. She returned carrying a shapeless bundle wrapped in a soiled cloth.

'I've told you before about dirt!' Helen said sharply, unwrapping the small, inert body of a male child. It was pale even for a Fan-Choan, and flaccid, its limbs hanging loosely as though the bones had never calcified. But it was still faintly warm.

'Geoff!' Helen called, seeing him beyond the carpet partition. 'Come and help me, please. All you others, excepting you, and you'—she grabbed Mahele's mother and younger sister—'out! Don't make that awful noise yet, either. Bring water. Plenty water. Cold and hot.'

Using a wide gourd and a large enamel pan as baths, one hot and one cold, Helen dipped the baby's body first in one, then the other. At the sixth cold dip the infant grew suddenly rigid and a thin cry escaped its lips.

'You see?' Helen almost shouted.

'It's stopped breathing again,' Geoff said later, as disappointed as she was.

But still Helen didn't abandon hope. Seizing a towel, she rubbed the baby briskly until she tired.

'You carry on, Geoff!'

He, too, rubbed, wondering where this slip of a girl found her faith. On the bed Mahele lay watching, propped on one elbow.

'I think I'm rubbing skin off,' Geoff announced.

Another thin cry sounded on the air. Helen seized the boy and swung him by the heels, slapping vigorously, and a thin trickle of slime emptied from the throat as the cry became stronger.

'There's my little love!' Helen cried, now cradling the infant in a towel in her arms. 'He'll do now, Geoff. You'll see—he'll do.'

'You mean he'll live?'

Helen was busy with small twists of cotton-wool, cleaning nostrils and eyes and ears.

'He's a beautiful boy, and all of eight and half pounds. I think his mum can do all that's necessary for him now.'

She laid the child in Mahele's waiting arms while the news crept out through the doorway to the women waiting outside. They looked astonished as Min Hana emerged, a little time later, to gasp in the air, the dentist sahib with her.

'That was a bad time while it lasted,' Helen announced.

'I simply can't believe it,' Geoff said, striking his brow. 'You're a revelation to me, Helen. You simply won't give in.'

'I hope not. There's a big difference between being dead and lying down, you know.'

'It's you, Helen. *You're* the marvel. I can't find words to—to—'

'To what, Geoff? I only did my job.'

'—to express my admiration for the way you do your job. Oh—what's the use? This is the only way to say what I've got to say.'

He seized her suddenly, rather roughly, and put his mouth hard against hers. For a moment she stood rigid, then she relaxed against him, giving way to reaction and tiredness and finding a certain sweetness in the stolen moment of surrender.

CHAPTER EIGHTEEN

By a mutual unspoken agreement, Helen and Geoff saw little of one another during the month which followed the birth of Mahele's son.

Helen told herself that to neglect her studies would be to overstrain the existing friendship between them. Friends, unlike lovers, had no actual need of physical contact, and could maintain their relationship without recourse to visual aids.

Geoff fancied he may have overplayed his hand as a friend in indulging that embrace, and though he admitted there had been decided mutual pleasure in it, there was the ever-present danger that a repetition of the event might well involve one—or both—in something deeper and less manageable. This was not likely to happen to him, but Helen must be treated fairly and not placed in a position where she might desire more of him than he was prepared to give.

As a woman he admired her tremendously, and since this was a new facet in his relationship with women he was inclined to become over demonstrative, as had been proved.

While lightnings played and thunders crashed, the inhabitants of the outlying islands were gathered into one community on Fan-Cho. The beach houses were emptied of their contents and deserted: larger family houses were constructed in the lee of the island's mountainous core, and all prepared for the worst the season could offer, this being a seventh year, and reputedly an ominous one.

The time of the monsoon was a trying one for Fan-Choans: for a while the visiting families were a novelty and all went well, then quarrels broke out inevitably. Young men argued and fought over the unmarried girls, and there was the odd case of infidelity by a married woman, which had, until ten years ago, always been a crime punishable by death. Nowadays, however, the wronged husband could divorce his wife by public denouncement and demand payment from the co-respondent for his sufferings. It was pathetic in these cases how a husband preferred several goats and chickens to the mother of his children. He could also claim his children once they were old enough to leave the mother, but more often than not was content to take his sons and teach them his trade, leaving the girls to the influences of the distaff side of the family.

On the whole, however, morality was high on Fan-Cho, and family feeling of great importance. The old were respected and cherished and deeply mourned when they died of extreme old age.

The *Madrassi Belle* called one more and announced she would be laying up for the rest of the monsoon. Heavier freighters using the trade routes would make a point of calling at Fan-Cho with mail and keep contact with the outside world. In an extremely formal letter, bearing Edward's signature, Helen was instructed to hold herself in readiness for three weeks' local leave now due to her. A locum would be coming out to take charge and she would be well advised to leave all advice and suggestions in writing as there would be no time for long discourse with her replacement.

Helen became quite excited at the thought of leave, and Fan-Cho suddenly seemed cramped and claustrophic. Her last leave had made no impression upon her at all, for there had been Edward to get over and her spirits, in consequence, weighted her down.

She went through her wardrobe time and again, wondering at her sudden interest in clothes. As her bank balance would have swollen considerably since her spell of duty on Fan-Cho, she felt free to indulge a spending spree, and dug out all the catalogues with which the United Indian Trading Company had inundated her by every mail.

She put off letting Geoff know of her intended departure as long as possible, then felt a stirring of conscience as Ling John arrived with a letter from his master.

It was an invitation to dinner.

'Dear Helen,

'I hope you don't think I have forgotten you, but I've been trying to cram a lot of work in before I go on leave. This may be at any moment—I sail on the next ship, in fact—so please join me at dinner this evening and tell me if there's anything I can do for you while I'm on the mainland . . .'

Helen's first reaction to this was shock followed by some irritation. He had taken the wind out of her sails with a vengeance. She had been nursing a scene in her mind in which she told Geoff she was going to leave Fan-Cho for a while, and in this scene his countenance visibly dropped before he could control it.

Now she acknowledged to herself that she had wanted Geoff to mind her going, whereas he was in reality full of his own plans for leaving her on the island, apparently not caring one jot or tittle about her so long as his own enjoyment was assured.

She presented herself for dinner wearing the yellow dress she knew he liked. His eyes certainly lit up when he saw her, but she was wary now, reminding herself of the long time that had passed since their last meeting.

'Snap!' she said during soup, causing him to drop his spoon and splash an otherwise immaculate shirt. 'I'm going on leave too. The next ship. We can't lose one another, can we?'

'Really?' he asked, mopping his lips with his napkin. 'Really!' he said again in a different tone.

She could sense he was thinking, but could not guess at his thoughts. They were not exactly complimentary to her and he was rather ashamed of them.

Could she possibly have found out he was due for leave and so arranged her own? He doubted it, but she might well have been sufficiently encouraged by his overtures of friendship to imagine she was the automatic selection of companion for him during his off-duty period.

'Where are you going?' he asked sharply.

'Oh, I don't know,' she shrugged. 'Where are *you* going?'

'What's that got to do with it?' he almost snapped. 'You must have plans! One doesn't just toss a coin on the dockside . . . !'

'Oh, but *I* do,' Helen said calmly. 'If it's heads I go to the Ghats in Travancore Anchel. I know some people up there with a plantation; tennis, swimming, polo—the lot. If it's tails I go touring—ancient monuments and the like.'

'That's what I'll be doing,' he said drily. 'I don't know any tea-planters.'

She flushed suddenly, having transcribed the whole of their conversation to measure up to his last remark.

'Geoff,' she said quickly, a high spot of colour staining each cheek, 'however the coin drops for me, you must do whatever you like. India's a big place. We're hardly likely to bump into one another once we're en-trained.'

He looked down, feeling bitterly ashamed.

'I know we're not, unless we arrange it,' he said quickly. 'Maybe it's not such a bad idea at that.'

'Stop!' she warned him. 'If the thought worried you a few minutes ago it's had no time to improve since. Why, I believe you were flattering yourself that I was *chasing* you! You have a very good opinion of yourself, Mr McLeod.'

He nodded ruefully.

'I deserve that, I suppose, and I'm sorry if I appeared to be a bighead. If I asked you nicely would you accompany me on a tour of ancient monuments?'

She was tempted by both the suggestion and his conciliatory tone, but her pride had suffered a severe blow.

'Thanks, but no,' she told him. 'We're friends, and friendship can survive a bit of separation. I'll wire my hosts in Travancore and you go touring. Will you be coming back to Fan-Cho?'

'Yes, but only to wind up my affairs. I should think eight weeks from now I'll be departing for the east coast. I'm to continue my researches among the poorer rice-eating classes. Sure you won't come with me on my travels as there's so little time left . . . ?'

She swallowed as she realised that after eight short weeks she was unlikely to see him again. It would seem lonely on Fan-Cho without him, but if it was only she who cared about this she must be careful to conceal it.

'I'm sure, Geoff,' she smiled a little mistily. 'You'll see much more if you travel alone. We'll have plenty to tell one another when we get back.'

'You're a nice little thing!' he said, covering her hand with his own in a sudden surge of affection. 'I sometimes think I haven't known any really nice women before, and I'm always looking for flaws—the catch—the gimme . . . Do you understand?'

'I think so,' she smiled, content to leave her hand where it was.

'You know, I shall always remember that wedding we went to, Helen. That was one of my happiest days. Nothing to it, really . . . I was with you, things were happening, the sky was blue and it was all so—so harmonious. Maybe that's not the exact word I'm looking for, but I'm trying to say that I discovered some of the best things in life are free on that day.'

'I think they all are,' she said wisely. 'The elements, health, love, friendship.'

He squeezed her hand, then his eye was caught by something beyond her.

'Yes, Wild Blossom?' he enquired, his gaze veiled and searching.

'Sorry to interrupt, Mr McLeod, but I have been working until now. May I go to my house?'

'Certainly. You shouldn't work so late, girl. Oh, Wild Blossom, you'll never believe this! Dr French is going on leave too. That's a coincidence, isn't it?'

'Isn't it?' Miss Huong said quietly. 'Goodnight.'

'I always feel I've offended that girl,' Helen said as the other vanished like a ghost. 'Am I imagining it, do you suppose?'

'Women are renowned for their intuition, aren't they?' he smiled. 'If that's the way Blossom affects you you'd better watch out. She once knifed a man who molested her.'

'But I don't intend to molest her,' Helen said simply.

It was three hours before Geoff escorted Helen back to her house. The evening had been spent in listening to records of classical music, though Geoff insisted he had

little ear for it except the 'tunes', and Helen had under-
taken to further his education on this subject before they
went their ways.

'A pity we haven't more time, isn't it?' he asked in
genuine regret. 'You could teach me musical appreciation and I could help you play chess.'

'I just beat you,' she said mock indignantly.

'I just let you,' he smiled aggravatingly. 'I've known
my grandma show more subtlety at draughts!'

'You mean—you mean—?' she asked grimly.

'Of course I mean—I mean—' he challenged her
afresh. 'You can't play chess for toffee!'

In another minute they were scuffling, breathing hard,
wrestling like children until they collapsed, breathless,
on the wide divan.

'Don't kiss me, Geoff!' Helen begged as he loomed
over her suddenly.

'How did you know I was going to?'

'I sort of sensed it.'

'Well—' he asked defensively, 'why mustn't I?'

'Because—friends don't kiss. Not when they're a man
and woman.'

'Are you afraid of the—other thing—between men
and women?'

'No, not if they're the right people for it.'

At this he released her, and now she was back at her
own house remembering, and rather wishing she hadn't
spoken that veto.

'If I didn't know myself better, I'd say I wanted Geoff
to fall in love with me,' she pondered as she lit a
kerosene lamp and went into her bedroom, 'but I
shouldn't think there's any real chance of it ever happening.'

'Are *you* a little bit in love with *him*?' her mirror asked
her as she brushed her long hair for the night. 'Aren't

you dreading the day he'll say goodbye to you for ever?'

'I won't answer that,' she said aloud. 'I won't think of it.'

She lifted the mosquito netting round her bed and dropped it behind her, then turned back the sheets. Next minute she froze with horror, for a yellow mottled coil of pure malevolence rose to challenge her presence.

Her hand still clutched the sheets and it was a question of her speed against the reptile's. She whipped the linen back in place, imprisoning him, and blundered back through the netting. The only heavy thing in the room that was portable was a small plaster bust of Apollo. Now Apollo attacked the writhing creature in the bed, smashing down again and again until it was still—and dead.

Helen could not face her bed that night. She lay on the bamboo divan in the living-room, trembling and sensing a rock cobra in every patch of shadow.

She had never before known one of the creatures to be in the vicinity of her bungalow, let alone find its way into her bed. Its venom would have given her a very bad week indeed, had it bitten her, and certainly caused her to postpone her leave.

It was not Bahadur who wakened her, but Blossom Huong. The Chinese girl was bending over the divan as she opened her surprised eyes.

'Yes, Miss Huong? Am I needed?'

The almond eyes wavered slightly.

'Oh! You're all right, Dr French?'

'I'm all right.' Suddenly Helen saw all. It was not by accident the rock cobra had found its way into her bed. '*I'm* certainly all right, Miss Huong, but you're very much all wrong. I think you would be well advised to stop worrying about Mr McLeod and myself. There's really nothing for you to worry about. Your attitude has been obvious to me for a long time. A pity if it should become as obvious to him, don't you think?'

Blossom could find no words. She turned and walked away, her hands clasped in the sleeves of her dress. Her very attempt at dignity, in the circumstances, was more than pathetic.

CHAPTER NINETEEN

On the high plateaux of Travancore Anchel the worst of the monsoon was over. The lower vertebrae of the Ghats, that mountainous region which is clothed in some of the densest of southern India's primeval jungle, kept the worst of the weather, at this season troubling the Bay of Bengal and the eastern states, away. Rain had refreshed the tea plantations and acres upon acres of new seedlings were now being planted out afresh in the damp, black soil of the district.

Travelling on the Madrassi State railways had been trying, to say the least, for until one had 'climbed' into the cooler air of the tableland the humidity was almost tangible. Helen, who had spent a couple of days in Madras, shopping, found herself suffering from the most debilitating inertia, scarcely able to summon up sufficient interest to call her carriage sweeper when she required a further change of linen and water to wash in. A day and a half later there had been further hazard: the train was now travelling over the highest part of the tableland and the air was consequently rarefied. Any exertion brought on palpitations to inexperienced travellers. Once it was known that Helen was a doctor she was kept busy, especially by the European contingent on the train.

Her own palpitations, which she understood, had to be forgotten as she staggered from carriage to carriage reassuring others.

She changed trains at the State line and then began to enjoy the wonderful scenery of Travancore Anchel, the cotton making a white mist like blossom in the valleys and the tobacco fields displaying young, firm, curled leaves like bracken fronds.

From the tobacco district the train progressed through a deeply scarred area, where manganese was being mined, to the tea gardens. Here, whether the owners were white or coloured, the outlook was decidedly European. White houses with spacious gardens appeared at intervals, and there were glimpses of well-dressed children at play, under the watchful eyes of attendant ayahs, and coolly-clad women carrying gay parasols and laughing at someone unseen or in the shadows of a spreading cedar. It all looked a splendid and extremely leisured way of life from the train, but Helen knew that tea-planters were really the head of small empires of dependents: on their judgment and acumen depended the management and their families, the backroom boys in the experimental laboratories, the foremen and their gangs, the vast army of pickers and planters. It was a responsible life and could easily make—or break—the economy of the country.

She was glad to detrain at Nachin, having spent three and a half days in travel, which, as is the way, already seemed eternity and left Fan-Cho aeons of time away in another dimension of her life. Only twice had she allowed herself to remember Geoff's cool, firm hand-shake as they parted outside the dock gates after dis-embarking from the cargo-passenger vessel *Indus* in its home port of Madras. She had hailed the American hotel taxi and he had said, 'Well, I'll shove off, then,' and as far as she knew he had 'shoved off' and could be anywhere by now.

The Marshalls were distant connections of her family, but family ties had been discounted by the friendship they had enjoyed with her parents. Mrs Marshall was, in fact, Helen's godmother, though she had always expressed regret that at the actual christening ceremony she had only been able to attend 'in spirit', as even in those days they had fallen under the spell of India and chosen to make their life there. Mr Marshall had progressed from a lowly position as estate clerk to general manager of a very fine plantation. The fact that the estate had changed ownership from an English aristocrat to a millionaire Parsee, who had never even seen the place, had fortunately not affected the Marshalls. They virtually ran Yan Udow as they pleased, and—being happy and satisfied with their lot—they had run it well. Everybody was happy at Yan Udow or Miles Marshall wanted to know the reason why.

'Helen, my dear!' Mary Marshall greeted, embracing her guest in genuine delight. 'How wonderful that you could come at this time! We have a few young folk staying with us, and you make the numbers right. We have an odd young man at the moment.'

Helen climbed thankfully into the car waiting outside the station. It was an open tourer and promised a cooling breeze.

'I'm not going to pester you with chatter until tomorrow morning, dear,' said Mrs Marshall firmly. 'I want all your news and so on, but it will do at breakfast. We'll have it in my room together. I've put you next door to me. You can come down to dinner or not, as you please. I know that after a three-hundred-mile journey in this country I simply desire oblivion for twelve hours.'

Helen was glad of such an understanding hostess, but once she had been introduced to her room and the immediate servants she found that two hours of oblivion apparently served her physical needs. She awoke at six, just before a glorious sunset, and walked out on to the balcony serving her room. Acres upon acres of tea were planted out in terraces on the sunny slopes of the nearer hills. Below them was a timber forest of teak and sandalwood, which gave the air a perpetual fragrance, as of sweet-smelling caskets and incense. The house itself was set in a pleasant, English-style garden, with pleasant English-looking flowers and lawns. A stream tinkled its way through the garden and paused to flood into a wide pool where India stepped in and grew lotus and pale lily cups among the flat green pads of their leaves. Beyond the garden, to the east, was a well-rolled lawn where the area managers gathered with their guests to play polo at the weekends.

Miles Marshall was proud of his polo ponies, which he bred as a sideline. When it was time to retire from tea-planting he had decided to make his pony stud his full-time occupation, and so remain in India all his life as a pensioner.

Helen had a bath and decided to show up for dinner. She was always inclined to be shy of meeting other young people, but putting if off only made it worse. She hoped the 'odd' young man wouldn't think it his painful duty to keep her constantly entertained. Already she knew what she wanted to do at Yan Udow: in the invigorating air she would study and fill her mind with the facts it refused to assimilate on Fan-Cho. It was sufficient to be in a paradise such as this without idling as well.

She wore a new evening dress in a flattering shade of turquoise blue and dressed her hair in a chignon.

'I'm getting vain in my old age,' she chided herself as she looked in the mirror, liking what she saw. 'I suppose I'd better show up at first gong for my aperitif—get the introductions over.'

She made her way downstairs at a little before eight, having heard Mrs Marshall descend earlier.

'Oh, you've decided to join us!' greeted the woman

gladly. 'I do hope you're rested, dear. You know our son Phil, don't you?'

'We met once,' Helen smiled, gazing up into the beaming face of the blond giant before her. 'We were about fourteen and Phil was a dreadful bully. He had me up and down trees I couldn't manage and over wired five-barred gates simply to prove girls were as good at such things as boys. My head and limbs were bloody and bowed before I'd completely vindicated my sex in his eyes.'

'That was the time I spent my vac with your folk in Sussex?' Phil asked, laughing. 'I shall promise not to "dare" you into any trouble this visit. May I introduce you to my wife, Candy?'

Candy Marshall was an American, dark-haired and twinkly-eyed.

'You must tell me all about that horrible boy you knew when we manage a get-together, honey,' she suggested. 'Having known Phil intimately for only six months I'm at the stage when I cain't hear enough about the darling.'

Helen next met an engaged couple, Fan Dailey and Richie Walmacott.

'He's our accountant,' Mrs Marshall afterwards explained, 'and Fan has come out to marry him. Unfortunately she's beginning to shilly-shally, wondering if she still feels the same about him. I've told her cold feet are usual in some brides, so I look to you to back me up, Helen. Richie would be devastated if she walked out on him now.'

'Isn't Candy the one to cheer her on?' Helen asked. 'Married life appears to agree with her.'

'I don't think so. Candy is an extrovert—comes out with everything before everybody. She makes marriage sound like a supercharged merry-go-round, and Fan is a quieter type, more like you. I think she feels she hasn't got for Richie what Candy has for Phil, and therefore it isn't enough. She feels she ought to be madly, demonstratively in love, but everybody isn't like that. Help her, Helen.'

'Is she approaches me, I'll try to advise her,' Helen agreed, 'but I'm not exactly an advertisement for connubial bliss myself, am I?' she smiled a little wryly. 'I'm still single at twenty-six and devoted to my work.'

'Which brings us to our remaining guest,' said Mrs Marshall, ambiguously, 'and he doesn't appear to be present. Oh, yes. There he is with Miles on the terrace. Come on!'

Helen gazed up at Geoff McLeod with her mouth a little open and her eyes disbelieving. Only when Mary Marshall managed to steer her husband away with an adroit, 'Well, I'll leave you two to get to know one another better,' did she recover the power of speech.

'I'm waiting, Geoff,' she said sternly, 'for your explanation of this. I left you outside Ali's Bar in Madras six days ago, remember? You were going that-a-way.'

She cocked her thumb over her shoulder.

Geoff set down his Martini with great delicacy on the stone balustrade.

'Really, Dr French, are you suggesting I'm *chasing* you? I won't strain gallantry by suggesting—as you did to me—that you have a very good opinion of yourself. Do you really think that as we made our salaams outside Ali's Bar I expected to meet you six days later four hundred miles away?'

'Don't strain my patience,' warned Helen. 'You had a general idea where I would be.'

'What's a mere general idea in a place the size of India?' he smiled as he raised his glass. 'It's fate, my girl. We must all bow . . .'

Helen, who had felt reasonably happy all day, now felt

something new, interesting and invigorating in the atmosphere.

Phil Marshall had dared her over gates to prove herself, now this man was throwing out a greater, weightier challenge to her sex.

As she raised her own glass, her eyes sparkled as she toasted, 'To fate, if that's what you call it! But what Mrs Marshall, my godmother, is going to think I wouldn't like to say!'

CHAPTER TWENTY

'ACTUALLY,' Geoff said, 'I mentioned to our hostess that a mutual friend had spoken of her in conversation, but she didn't ask who. I suppose there'll have to be a confessional now?'

'That's rather difficult,' Helen pronounced, 'because I don't know why you're here, do I? I didn't tell you where the Marshalls lived, I'm sure.'

'No, you didn't. I saw your man, Bahadur, on the train to the north and he gave me your address.'

Helen still frowned.

'But why should you want it? We had only just separated . . .'

'I know. Quite frankly, I was sorry to see you go. I felt I had somehow offended you, as the atmosphere between us on the ship appeared somewhat strained.'

'You idiot! I wasn't offended at all. I didn't want to be under your feet all the time.'

'I think that's the trouble. We've been awfully anxious not to create wrong impressions, and that's just what we've done!'

'I don't understand . . .' Helen frowned.

'We've created wrong impressions by the dozen. At least, I have. I've kept away from you at times when I wanted to be with you. That was a wrong impression for a start. Why shouldn't I be with you if I enjoy your company? What's wrong in that?'

Helen was silent, trying to interpret his words correctly.

'Unless, of course, you don't enjoy being with me to

an equal degree?' he went on urgently. 'Actually, I was taking that for granted. Bigheaded of me again, I suppose?'

'No,' Helen said quietly. 'I enjoy your company, Geoff. But how much do we tell our hosts? Mrs Marshall may—er—be inclined to read more into our friendship than exists. She's a romantic, you know.'

'You tell her what you like. I'll back you up.'

'Then you did actually come to Travancore to see me?'

'Absolutely, if I could. I flew here the day after we landed. Of course there *are* some sights to see hereabouts if I hadn't made a hit with the Marshalls.'

Squeezing her arm happily and contentedly, as though flying four hundred miles to see a girl he had only just left was an everyday occurrence, Geoff McLeod led her in to dinner without more ado.

Helen rather dreaded the morning's tête-à-tête with her godmother, but all was made easier for her than she had imagined.

'What do you think of Mr McLeod, dear? He's a dentist—or did you know?'

'Yes, I knew. Actually he's much more than that. He's a dental scientist. I've met him before. It was a surprise seeing him here, of course.'

'It must have been. I forget how we came to know him. People say "Be sure and call on the Marshalls", knowing our capacity for entertaining, and of course they do. I thought him a very nice young man. Are you *quite* heart-free, Helen?'

A pause, and then, 'Yes, I think so. I buried an affair quite recently.'

'The older you get the more selective you become. At twenty all personable young men are possible husbands, but at twenty-six you'll be lucky to find one in ten you could look at twice. You and Mr McLeod should find you have a lot in common.'

'Now, now!' Helen chided. 'There you go! Geoff and I are good friends, and nothing more is likely between us.'

'Unlikely things happen when least expected. But I'll say no more. I have one unwilling bride on my hands and I don't want two. Feel free to do as you like, Helen, but do try to keep Mr McLeod from feeling out of things. There's just one thing: keep yourself free for the estate ball in the recreation hall on Friday next. It's our turn to give it. I'll expect you to help with the flowers.'

'Delighted,' smiled Helen, and made her escape.

She had bathed and was dressing when a woman servant tapped on her door and handed her a note.

'From Missie-sahib Dailey, Doctor-sahib,' the woman bowed, and slipped away again.

Helen unfolded the sheet of note-paper in puzzlement and read:

'Dear Dr French,
    'I think I have a fever. Would you call and see me, please? My room is at the end of the corridor and has a red-painted door.'

It was signed 'Frances Dailey.'

Helen finished dressing in a cool cotton frock, blue with white piping, then pocketed a thermometer and carried her stethoscope in her hand. For one suffering from a fever Miss Dailey had a remarkably neat hand and a facility for giving detailed direction. Helen found the room the English girl occupied without any trouble whatsoever.

Frances Dailey writhed and tossed in the bed as Helen entered the room, after tapping, but on the whole the bedclothes were neat and trim.

'Don't talk yet, Miss Dailey,' advised Helen, popping the thermometer in the other's mouth and putting the cool palm of her hand on the other's brow. There was some heat but definitely no fever. The thermometer read normal.

'Now,' Helen began, sitting on the edge of the bed, 'what's the trouble?'

'I—I thought you could tell me that,' said the other. 'I feel frightfully hot and confused and I haven't slept a wink all night. My throat feels dry and—'

'Say "Ah",' instructed Helen.

The other did so.

'Nothing to worry about. I would say you're drinking a little too much in the evenings and maybe not eating enough. That would account for both the mental confusion and the dryness in the throat. Shall I listen to your chest?'

Frances Dailey unfastened the ribbons of her night-dress and then grew suddenly limp.

'Oh, what's the use? I know I'm not ill. I'm simply in the biggest blue funk of my life, Dr French. I—I suppose you know why?'

'Is it something to do with a wedding?'

'Yes. I know it's rotten of me, but I can't face marrying Richie next week. I simply can't!'

'Then I should tell him without more ado,' Helen advised. 'It'll be a blow, but the sooner he starts getting over it the sooner he'll be free to think of somebody else. Men get over these things quicker than women.'

Frances looked dumbstruck.

'I didn't say I don't love Richie,' she protested, 'simply that I can't marry him next week. I want to go home and get married to him later. I *do* love him. Desperately.'

Helen smiled a little wryly.

'Oh, come, my dear. You can't expect me to believe you care about someone you can't bear the idea of living with? Don't be absurd!'

'But I do. You put things very awkwardly, if you don't mind my saying so, Dr French. I wouldn't hurt Richie for the world. I simply want somebody like you to tell him that I'm—er—not very well just now and it would be better to put things off for twelve months. I don't think that's asking a lot.'

'I'm beginning to feel sorry for Richie,' Helen declared, realising she must be cruel to be kind. 'Of all the girls who would have given their ears to come out and be married in a fairy tale setting like this, he has to pick *you*. If I tell your fiancé anything it will be that you're a ridiculous neurotic and he's well rid of you. Grow up, girl! Seize your happiness! You can't put love off for twelve months and expect it to be the same. If you don't go through with this marriage, as arranged, Richie will learn to hate you for what you've done to him. You're as good as telling him you prefer your parents' guardianship to his. What are you afraid of? Life? Love? Love-making?'

'I wanted my mother here,' Fan said desperately. 'If only my mother could have been here—'

'I can tell you all you want to know from a physiological point of view,' Helen said more kindly, 'and one usually says goodbye to one's mother when one says hello to one's husband. That's life. One must grow up and mature. Marriage is nature's way of turning the girl into the woman—the ideal way. No one has thought of a better way yet.'

'But you're not married . . . ?'

'No. But that doesn't mean I don't know what I'm missing, does it? I know if I was in love with someone who loved me, and my wedding was next week, I'd be the happiest girl in the world, and utterly conceited.'

'But wouldn't you want your mother here?'

'That wouldn't be of primary importance. Anyway, I had to say goodbye to my mother many years ago. She's dead. No matter how dear they are, parents have a habit of dying before their children, and if the child is unmarried, life can be very lonely and bleak.'

Fan said, 'I suppose I've been looking on the grim side and magnifying all possible snags quite out of proportion. When I was at home I know I longed for Richie more than I could bear. I used to snap at Mother then, and offend her. I seem to have reversed the procedure since I've been here.'

'Make no mistake,' Helen warned, 'you have to love a man before all others if you expect a happy marriage. Richie must come first, not your family.'

'May I think over what you've said, Dr French? I'm sorry for involving you, but you've made me see many things much more clearly. I couldn't bear to lose Richie, you know. I never thought in my blind panic that I might do just that so very easily. Thank you so much.'

Helen rose.

'I do hope you'll be happy, my dear, however you decide.'

'Thank you. Thank you very much.'

As Helen went down the wide staircase she met Geoff McLeod.

'Where have you been? I've been looking all over for you.'

'I've been giving advice to the young-in-love, if you must know.'

'You've been giving *what*? I shouldn't think you knew much about *that* subject.'

'Youth, or love, Mr McLeod?'

'Both, Dr French,' he bowed mockingly. 'Friendship's your great forte, remember? And one can be any old age for that!'

CHAPTER TWENTY-ONE

THE bridegroom-to-be, in the Marshall's house party, was pathetically touched by his beloved's remarkably swift recovery from whatever it was that had been debilitating her ever since her arrival on the subcontinent. Blind, as all lovers are blessed to be, he had believed her when she said she was unsure of her fitness to go through with the marriage as arranged. Blighted he was by the thought, but he did not blame her, and having practically reconciled himself to a further period of bachelor living, he was delighted when Fan not only told him one evening she was going to marry him, but on the date they had previously decided upon, then only four days distant.

'You're sure you feel up to it, darling?'

'I'm certain. Dr French gave me a tonic, and—' her voice was lost in a sudden, glorious, vigorous embrace.

'God bless Dr French!' said Richie as they both regained their breath, having eyes for none but each other. 'I must say you look different, my sweet. I—we almost seem to belong together now, this minute, without any marriage ceremony.'

'But we'll have it just the same, won't we, Richie?'

'Yes, darling. I can be patient a little longer.'

'Lovers are a bit embarrassing to have around,' pronounced Geoff McLeod as he walked past with Helen. 'The young marrieds are as bad. You and I are the only members of this household not engaged in a necking session. I even saw our hosts indulging in a middle-aged cuddle.'

Helen saw herself and her escort reflected dimly in the waters of the lily pool, and paused.

'We could soon remedy that,' she observed coolly.

Geoff paused as though tugged to a standstill.

'What did you say?' he asked blankly.

Helen felt nervous and mischievous at the same time.

'I said we would soon remedy the fact of not being as—as pleasurably occupied as the others appear to be.'

Geoff's silence was the only ponderous element in the ephemeral airiness of the highland night.

'Do I understand you aright, Helen?' he asked sententiously at last. 'Are you now inviting me to—to kiss you?'

'Honestly, Geoff,' she said in mock exasperation, 'I wouldn't want you to do anything against your principles. Prig!' she added aside, with a sigh.

'I'm not a prig!' he told her, whipping her round to face him. 'That last time I was going to kiss you it was you put the red light on. Remember?'

'I remember,' she said with some irritation, 'but if you were a real man of flesh and blood I wouldn't have been able to stop you, if kissing me had been your intention. Anyway, that was a long time ago and we were practically alone together. This is different.'

'How different?'

Her eyes lit up with two flames of sheer annoyance.

'We see everybody else behaving normally in this romantic, relaxed atmosphere. Obviously they see us, also, *not* behaving normally. How do you think I feel?'

He began to see what she was driving at.

'You mean you feel neglected?'

'I shouldn't have to put it into words. I *look* neglected, no matter how I may feel, and it makes me resemble somebody's ageing spinster aunt. Do you think I'll sue you for breach of promise, or something, if you kiss me occasionally?'

He came back with an unexpected broadside.

'I don't know how high a value you place on your kisses, do I? Are they—as the Americans put it—for free?'

She looked at him for a moment as though he had struck her, then passed him quickly and disappeared behind a hedge of hibiscus.

'Helen!' he called, hearing her feet tapping ahead of him in their high-heeled shoes as she ran. 'Come back, darling I didn't mean it!'

On she hastened, however, through the formal gardens and out into the wilder growth of the plateau.

He heard her for a while, then as the ground fell away for thousands of feet ahead of him, showing a moon-illuminated valley, glistening with streams below, he could hear her no more.

'Helen!' he called anxiously.

Wherever she blundered now there was danger: it was bad enough in daylight when one could see the precipitous tracks in all their tortuous clarity.

'Oh, Helen!' he called again. 'Don't fall, darling!'

He parted the curtaining lacery of aspen leaves and saw her; she was standing leaning rigidly against a natural monolith of grey, red-veined rock, apparently looking down into the valley.

'Helen,' he said gently, 'why didn't you answer me?'

Her answer was in the eyes she unwillingly turned on him, for they were the eyes of a stranger.

He was aware of a new and bitter sensation pumping lead into his heart: he felt an awareness of loss, the tragedy of which would strike him harder when he had had time to realise it.

'Helen?' his voice questioned her, and his arms slid

round her in a kind of desperation. 'I didn't mean to offend you,' he said urgently. 'I simply couldn't believe—'

'—that I was making myself so cheap?' she finished in an unnatural, dry-sounding voice.

'No. You couldn't be cheap, Helen. Don't put words into my mouth.'

'But when one is reduced to offering one's kiss "for free" . . .'

'Please—please don't remember that or hold it against me. I didn't know what I was saying.'

'I think you always know what you're saying, Geoff. You've made it quite clear on numerous occasions that I don't have any effect on your emotions, so can't claim that you were at all confused by my clumsy, unfeminine invitation.'

'This is all wrong, Helen,' he said, shaking her a little. 'We shouldn't be like this.'

'I would prefer to endure my humiliation alone,' she said dully. 'Please go back to the house.'

'No. Not leaving you thinking the wrong things. I would like to kiss you, Helen. Honestly. Please ask me again.'

'Kiss me, if you want to.'

He sought her lips clumsily and feverishly, hoping to find the warmth of the friend, at least. But he might have been kissing the face of the rock behind. Her lips were obedient but without enthusiasm: when he returned more vigorously to the assault they were still soft, moist and parted, but dead.

'Not very successful, was it?' she asked as she released herself. 'That should teach us not to step out of our context in future!'

Geoff McLeod scarcely slept all that night, and when he

did, his dreams were a confusion of miserable and fevered activities. He was either charging off on leaden feet in pursuit of something he could never hope to catch, or awaiting with an exaggerated sensation of utter hopelessness, for someone or something which failed to arrive. In his wakeful moments he was repining something which could well be lost to him, and that something was Helen's friendship.

At times he felt desperate about this, and wanted to rise and seek Helen out to gain her assurance that all would be the same between them on the morrow.

He knew, however, in his heart that things could never be the same again, and in one way he didn't want them to be. In his arms, in that unhappy hour on the plateau, he had held an ice princess, whose warm life his own thoughtlessly cruel words had sucked away, without reason other than he had been playing for time, his own state of mind distinctly unbalanced by her apparently heedless badinage. That ice princess he must restore to her former glowing, confident, bounding life, and then, in her kiss, he would find the answer to all that was sorely troubling his usually disciplined mental processes.

Why—he often asked himself—had he rushed to the airport in Madras and bribed an official to wangle him a passenger seat on the already overcrowded plane bound for Travancore Anchel? Why had the sight of Helen's leaving him for anywhere, lately, have disturbed the balance of his otherwise untrammelled days? Why did he push her from him roughly—savagely, almost—when she seemed to be coming too close to him on occasions? Could one seek, without the inevitability of finding, and remain happy? What did he want of this slight, sweet, red-haired girl whom he had admittedly followed across a continent so as to miss no more of her company than could be helped? Did he want her arm always tucked chummily through his as they walked with averted eyes past declared lovers? Was contentment of mind in her avowed friendship and what went with it; letters when they were apart; a shared dinner-table and unimpassioned conversation when they were not?

'How dull all that seems now!' Geoff sat up in bed to declare at four o'clock in the morning. 'Why don't I admit I'm in love with the girl and do something about it before it's too late? Why don't I?'

Now that the rash was out he suddenly felt better.

'Of course I'm in love with her!' he continued in relief. 'That's it! I thought love was the way I felt about Celeste, but now I realise her appeal was almost wholly physical. That last evening, when all was over between us, I could hardly bear to be with her. But with Helen I can't bear *not* being with her, which is why I'm here at the very moment. She must have thought I was an odd character, coming here and wangling my way into her friends' household, and all for the privilege of insulting and humiliating her when she was trying to be more friendly than usual. Will she ever forgive me? That's the question. I want to tell her over and over again I love—love—love her, but will she believe me? Does she care about me in the same way?'

The last question brought a host of doubts crashing like bricks about his ears, for he did not read into Helen's playful suggestion that they kiss—to be in the fashion—an undying declaration of her devotion.

He was sunk, while she was probably sleeping soundly by now, his offence forgotten if not forgiven.

'I wish it was time to get up!' he thought miserably. 'Just seeing her would be better than this—this desperate uncertainty.'

The object of his now declared affections at that moment awoke from an uneasy sleep to remember a pair of lips upon her own, demanding what it was no longer hers to bestow.

'Oh, Geoff!' she sighed miserably into her pillow. 'It all started as a game and ended so horribly! I wish I wasn't even your friend now. I wish I didn't know you.'

CHAPTER TWENTY-TWO

THE bride wore real orange blossom to keep her veil in place. Helen took the heady cluster of blooms from the gardener, still heavy with dew, and wove it round wire into a coronet fit for a queen.

'I didn't know you were good at that sort of thing,' Geoff said from behind her as she worked in the loggia before the sun became too hot.

'I'm not all that good,' she said politely, with a cool little smile in his direction. They had been extremely polite with one another for the past two days. 'It's just that I have the smallest hands and am expected to be skilful owing to my job. These blossoms bruise very easily if mishandled. The scent is overpowering, isn't it?'

'Wonderful and exotic.' He stooped to smell them. 'I didn't know oranges grew hereabouts.'

'They're smaller than the Mediterranean type, and not so juicy as the African. Neither are they as interesting as mandarins. But orange blossom is wonderful the world over, isn't it?'

'Wouldn't you like to be doing that job for yourself?' he asked with deliberate casualness, sitting some distance away from her.

'You mean making a bridal wreath?' she laughed lightly. 'I'm sure I'd be in too much of a tizzy to do it for myself.'

'Why?'

'Well, I presume I'd be madly in love and desperately nervous.'

'And can you visualise the probability taking place?'
She laughed again.

'My getting married? No, I can't, frankly.'

'Does no one fit the bill for you?'

She darted a glance at him.

'In my present orbit, no. But I'm quite happy, Geoff,' she suddenly warned him, 'don't be so obvious. You owe me nothing, so I'd rather you didn't follow me around like a whipped dog trying to pay it back. Do you understand me?'

'Perfectly,' he said heartily. 'I offended and I'm not to be forgiven.'

'Rubbish! There's nothing to forgive. I don't know why there's such a change in you lately.'

'Don't you?' he desperately appealed.

'No,' she snapped. 'It's not like you to walk around as though apologising for your very existence. I liked you better as you were.'

'I think I liked myself better as I was, but unfortunately I have to live with myself as I am.'

He rose and went away, leaving Helen feeling vaguely unsettled.

'Because I made a fool of myself the other evening it doesn't mean I have to be reminded of it eternally, or does it?' she pondered darkly. 'Geoff looks at me as though *he* was the offender, and he's so anxious for my future all of a sudden. I wish I could fall in love with somebody, to set his mind at rest, or at least indulge in a mild flirtation. The poor boy thinks he has damned my feminine self-assurance for all time, and I'm not sure he isn't right!'

One of the wedding guests was a nice-looking fair-haired young man with the brick-red countenance of the Englishman who refuses to wear a head covering in the noonday sun of India. He had been working for months on a new plantation and been denied the society of members of the opposite sex. He was immediately drawn to Helen as a bee to the honey-pot, and had an easy, relaxed, masculine assurance about him which caused Geoff agonies of jealousy.

Colin Garson attended Helen faithfully throughout the morning, her laughter rang and her eyes danced when in his company. Mrs Marshall had ordered a buffet lunch to precede the afternoon ceremony, and it was Colin who filled Helen's plate and carried it to her on the terrace with an accompanying pleasantry which once again made her laugh.

Geoff made a miserable third to this trio, sitting dumbly like a skeleton at the feast.

'Cheer up, McLeod,' said Colin brightly as he raised his glass of beer in salute. 'You might have been the bridegroom today: we who are still at large must stand together, what?'

'Cheers!' Geoff said gloomily.

'Tell me—' Colin said conspiratorially—'do *you* know anything about this, dear charmer here?'

Helen was smiling indulgently as she bit into a sandwich.

'Hardly anything.' Geoff snubbed the other, hoping he was hurting Helen a little too.

'I can't believe she hasn't a swain sitting somewhere. I just can't.' His hazel eyes absorbed Helen's beauty and blushes, for beautiful she was under such open masculine scrutiny. 'She's too good to be true. I swear I shan't notice the bride while this girl's around.'

'Stop it, Colin!' Helen adjured, as though she had known the fellow for months instead of hours. 'This is Fan's day and we simply don't exist. Remember that, or I shan't sit beside you in church.'

Geoff almost protested at that moment, then remembered he had merely assumed Helen would be accompanying him to the church. He had failed to ask her formally.

'I'll behave,' Colin said mock-humbly. 'But tell me, dearest lady, do we exist when all this business is over?'

'Of course we do,' Helen chuckled. 'It's the ball tonight. Do you dance, Colin?'

'Fairly efficiently.'

Helen turned, catching Geoff's frowning countenance unawares.

'Do *you* dance?' she asked politely.

'Fairly inefficiently,' he said nastily, and excused himself as he rose and strode away.

'Tell me,' Colin asked conversationally, 'would I be intruding in any way between him and you?'

'No,' Helen scorned. 'You can call us friends and colleagues. That's all.'

'Then why does he hate these poor innocent guts, my sweet?'

'You're imagining things. Weddings have a morbid effect on some people. I should think Geoff's feeling a bit depressed. I like weddings myself.'

'So do I. Other people's. When I fall it'll be for someone like you, dear doctor, so be warned! I'll need dragging to an altar, though.'

Leaning across swiftly, he dropped a light kiss on her cheek and then paused to see how she would take his action.

'That isn't where I'll be kissing you tonight, my sweet,' he whispered, encouraged by her silence.

'Isn't it?' she asked, brightly, fully aware that Geoff was still watching and glowering from a distance. 'That remains to be seen. Will you excuse me for a moment? I want to see if I can help anyone.'

She passed Geoff without a word and left him feeling as empty as a barrel drained of wine.

'Dearly beloved, we are gathered together here in the sight of God, and in the face of this congregation . . .'

The familiar words rang out, and it was difficult to imagine this wedding was not taking place in a village church at home, with the green fields stretching into the distance and the well-wishers waiting to throw confetti on the happy couple.

'I require and charge you both . . .'

They were serious words, Helen decided, and not to be heard lightly or used frivolously.

She had already released her hand meaningly from Colin Garson's seeking grip.

'This isn't the cinema,' she had reproved him, and 'Sorry, old thing,' he had replied merrily. 'When can we do a flick together?'

'. . . As ye shall answer at the dreadful day of judgment . . .'

Terrible and thought-provoking words. You simply couldn't marry the wrong person and use this time-honoured service to do it. It would be committing perjury.

Helen noticed Geoff sitting stiffly two rows in front. A funny little pain hurt her heart as she saw him so obviously alone and looking attentive and remote. She wished now she was sitting beside him and not Colin, who apparently didn't take anything very seriously. Geoff's hair was thick and black and his neck was brown against the white of his collar. She noticed his ear, as he turned slightly, and it was shaped like a map of Africa and lay flat against his fine head.

'Wilt thou have this woman to thy wedded wife . . . ?'

What a moment for Geoff to turn and regard her, as

though pulled by the magnetism of her gaze! For a second their eyes locked in a swift communion, only to be torn apart as Richie's voice could he heard emotionally admitting, 'I will'.

Fan was utter composure in comparison, and Helen wondered if *she* had really been instrumental in bringing this wedding about. The frightened, confused girl, hiding behind the symptoms of hypochondria, could scarcely be this statuesque young woman who was now bolstering her groom, with her love and understanding, at the altar steps.

Now Fan Dailey wore a wedding ring and this night would see her a true wife.

Helen's sigh was misinterpreted by her hedonistically pursuited companion.

'Some people like to do things the hard way,' he whispered in her ear, 'but light pursuits are more in my line.'

'Do be quiet, Colin!'

'You're resisting me, Helen. I shall kiss you in a minute.'

'You'll do no such thing . . . !'

One or two people turned on hearing the brief scuffle in the fifth pew and Helen's cheeks were scarlet with embarrassment.

Geoff's disapproval accompanied her as they knelt in prayer.

She was glad when the rest of the service was over and Colin was at least outside the church with his nonsense. Obviously he was—as he had stated—a companion fitted only for the lighter pursuits of life. Now that she knew, she could arrange her dalliance with him in the right settings, and avoid him at other times. The fellow resembled champagne and made her feel gay and rather carefree, but when one needed true nourishment for soul or spirit, he left one with a feeling of unsatisfied hunger and emptiness.

The happy couple were speeded on their way to a honeymoon tour of Sri Lanka, and then—as is usual—everyone felt rather flat for a while.

'After your nap you'll help me with the flowers in the Club hall, won't you, Helen?' asked Mrs Marshall, looking extremely hot and relieved that the wedding was off her capable hands.

'Of course I will.'

'The servants will bring char to your room. I insist on you lying down for at least an hour. Do you hear?'

Helen smiled, squeezing the other's shoulder as they went upstairs together.

'I'm the doctor hereabouts and *I* insist you have at least two hours' rest. I'll go along and start the decorations, so don't worry. Somebody will help me.'

She took off the blue silk dress she had worn for the wedding and flung herself on her bed to cool off. Her thoughts should have been untroubled, a wedding over and a night of dancing ahead, but instead she felt a sense of oppression as though her life was proving ineffectual and frustrated.

'I'm just not cut out for a social existence,' she sighed into her pillow. 'Very little soon palls with me, and I haven't even glanced at a text book since I've been here. I think I'll be glad to get back to work. It won't be long now.'

CHAPTER TWENTY-THREE

THE Club hall stood in the estate village, next to a fine swimming-pool, which was, this evening, quite deserted. Neat little terraces of employees' houses looked out on to a large square, nicely dissected into playgrounds, thoroughfares and gardens. The labourers too had their own swimming-pool, a natural tank which had been cleared and chlorinated for their use.

This evening, however, they were all out in force watching the sahibs and their memsahibs arriving for the annual estate ball. There was no envy in them, in fact they took a familiar interest in the Europeans as they drew up in their shining cars outside the club-house.

'That's my sahib!' or, 'There's the Northern Area Manager's memsahib. She has four fine children. Little devils, they are!'

Of course this was all spoken in the district dialect, and passed on from one to another.

'Four children? The memsahib I work for has none. She says children get sick in India. How did *we* grow up, then? Eh?'

There was laughter at this.

'White people are comical, Chandrassi-lal, especially when they speak our language. My manager thinks he's a very good Hindustani speaker. He said to me yesterday, "Why you not work like half a man sometimes? All the time you work like two men!" I said, "Right, sahib. I take holiday and work like half a man in future." When he gets mad I tell him what he said. Now he expects me to work like *two* men, though, so I did myself no good. It's funny, when you think of it.'

There was a sudden panic among the watching women, clustered together away from their men-folk.

'Is the doctor here? Where is the doctor-sahib?'

'Why? What is wrong?'

'Illala's small son found his father's knife. Now his finger is hanging off. He bleeds.'

There was a rushing of bare brown feet to the European club-house doorway, a small child was screaming in terror as it blindly held a practically severed finger in place with its uninjured hand.

'Doctor!'

'*Doctor*! the cry went up.

The estate doctor had not yet arrived: instead a slim young woman dressed in a froth of lavender tulle came forward, announcing, 'I am a doctor. What has happened?'

One woman gabbled at her, another was kissing her feet in their silver brocaded shoes.

'Don't do that, please. Bring the boy into this room here.'

The distressed child, now faint with shock and terror, was laid on a table where ladies had recently been dumping their cosmetics while they made up for the occasion.

Helen sought in her bag for clean gauze, antiseptics.

'The best thing which could have happened is that he kept his finger in place like this. We may save it for him.'

While native women watched and moaned, and one European lady swooned gracefully at the sight of blood, Helen bathed, stitched and dressed the wound.

'He should be all right in the morning,' Helen told the mother. 'He needs sleep. Take him to the clinic for Dr West to see it tomorrow.'

'Thank you, Memsahib-doctor. Thank you.'

'And knives out of reach in future, eh?'

'On my life, Memsahib. God bless you.'

Helen felt somewhat exalted for having been called upon in this emergency. It was work she was missing, she told herself, as she went out into the hall she had recently helped to turn into a bower of exotic blossoms, and was immediately swept into a quickstep by Colin Garson.

'What was all the row outside, dearest? A massacre?'

'No, you idiot. A small boy had been experimenting with a knife. I stitched him.'

'Garn!' scoffed Colin, holding her away from him for a moment to regard her. 'You don't mean to tell me you're a real, practising medico? "I swear by Hippocrates . . ." and all that?'

'Of course I am. Have been for years.'

'For years, says Grandma! You really know what makes us tick over, then? I'll have to watch you, young lady. A male's blood pressure is obviously no mystery to the likes of you, and I suppose love is just a chemical formula, eh?'

'I'm a great believer in love.'

'Then why haven't you succumbed before now? Come and tell me among the roses.'

He whirled her out of doors into a terraced garden. In the background a fountain played and splashed diamonds as the rising moon caught the water in its pale light.

'I like dancing,' Helen said quickly, feeling the man beside her slipping into a new rôle as easily as the chameleon changes its colour. 'Let's go back inside.'

'Time for forfeits, Dr Helen.' An arm pinioned her against a stone balustrade. 'Colin demands two kisses per dance. Pay up?'

She didn't answer. It all seemed rather silly. This man

didn't realise he had the wrong girl if it was trifling he wanted. She knew what his kiss would be like before she experienced it—smooth, urbane, meaningless.

'My waltz, I believe, Helen?' came Geoff's voice from near at hand. 'You *will* excuse us, Garson?'

Colin was left fuming, and on the dance floor Helen felt herself held just right—not too close—and slipping into a perfect, sure-footed rhythm.

'Thank you, Geoff. Thank you,' she said when it was over, clapping hard and hoping for an encore. 'You dance very well.'

'Thank *you*,' he bowed, and as a portly planter came up, he stepped aside, and allowed her to be swept away, albeit her gaze was on him, questioningly, as she peered over her partner's shoulder.

Once Colin had re-established himself with her, however, he stood aside for no one.

'The more you give me the slip, Helen, the more I'll chase you,' he warned. 'It may be your doctor's training, but you know how to handle me to a T. I'm becoming quite proprietorial about you.'

She managed to keep him at bay, away from dim corners and moonlit terraces, until after supper. Then he told her Mrs Marshall wanted to see her, led her away into the garden and tugged her down on to a low stone seat beside the fountain.

'You deceived me, Colin! Let me go!' she said in annoyance, struggling to sit upright.

'Now don't go all virtuous on me, darling. You're a woman of the world. I'm going to kiss you and make you like it.'

In vain she struggled, loth to make a scene. He was too strong for her.

'I hate you for this.' Her voice trembled. 'You're making me feel cheap and nasty.'

'You shouldn't have led me on, love. I'm raw spirit and you're fire. Now be still.'

'Stand up!' commanded a new voice.

Colin looked up in amazement.

'Good lord, McLeod! I'm getting sick of the sight of you!'

'Ditto. Stand up.'

'Are you going to knock my block off, or something?'

'Either that or duck you in the fountain. Take your pick.'

'Don't make any trouble, Geoff,' Helen said, still sounding shaken. 'Let him go.'

'Let me go?' Colin demanded. 'What the hell am I supposed to have done? Was I harming you in any way, Helen?'

'No, I suppose not. I'm just not that sort of girl.'

'So clear off,' shouted Geoff.

Colin looked for a moment outraged and angry, then thought better of making a fresh outburst and stalked away.

'Now I feel awful!' Helen decided, her head in her hands. 'As Colin said, he didn't really hurt me, only my dignity.'

'I don't want to hear any details, thank you,' Geoff cut her short, 'and in case you too think I was playing peeping Tom, you're wrong. I was here first.'

'You didn't ask me to dance again,' she complained after a few minutes' silence.

'I didn't feel like dancing. I was going back to the house, actually.'

'No. Don't go, Geoff.'

He looked at her sharply.

'Now don't tell me you missed me?'

'Yes. Yes, I did. I'm afraid I'm not very good in a crowd.'

'You appeared to be doing all right to me.'

'I was *trying* to do all right. It may have looked like the real thing.'

'Will you come for a stroll with me? I'd rather like to talk to you.'

'Certainly.'

He offered his arm and she took it, glad of its familiarity, knowing it wouldn't let her down or change—chameleon-like—into something different.

They walked for about half a mile in complete silence, then Geoff paused and drew her to face him. The moment was charged with seriousness.

'This has to be the time and place,' he said, 'though I would rather we had been together on Fan-Cho at this moment. I love you, Helen. I think I've always loved you, though you won't believe that. Now, however, the fact is no secret to me and gives me no peace. I know you're completely heartfree, which is why I have kept silence this long, but I can't answer for my actions when I see other men mauling you. I wanted to do murder back there.'

He closed his eyes and his voice had wavered to a standstill.

'Geoff!' she cried out.

'Don't speak yet,' he warned her. 'I haven't finished. Knowing your innate kindness of heart, I should hate you to answer me in kindness. I want something much more—or nothing. You've gaily tossed your favours here, there and everywhere, lately, and I, blind fool! was the only one to question them, though I shall hope for them as my right if your regard grows towards me. If it doesn't grow, however, into what you and I know to be true and whole love, then refuse me, Helen, for both our sakes.'

There was a pregnant pause.

'I'm sorry if I've shocked you, my darling,' he continued in a whisper. 'Good old Geoff, your friend, declaring himself like this. I can tell you I'm shaken too. But you'll think it over, won't you, and tell me when to abandon all hope?'

Her eyes were starred with tears.

'Don't cry for me, old thing!' he said more gaily. 'One doesn't die of these maladies. I wonder if I could have that kiss now, for goodnight?'

She raised trembling lips, and felt the gentle firmness of his, passionless, humble and yet vibrant with promise.

'Goodnight, Geoff,' she said softly, not knowing yet what the reaction to his declaration would be.

Geoff loved her. It couldn't be true! He had always shied away from any suggestion of a relationship closer than friendship, and yet their friendship had worn gloves, simply because it was afraid (if that was the word) of any direct contact.

Hadn't this been written in the stars from the beginning? Was not the blind seeking-out in which they had both indulged a facet of human love?

'I feel happy,' Helen declared deliriously, as she undressed later, 'as though all my troubles were over. I don't need to think it over when my heart knows the truth. I love Geoff. I love—love—love him. What's more, I'll tell the darling—first thing in the morning!'

Colin was returning from an early swim when she arose and went out of doors.

'Old thing!' he called after her. 'Sorry if I offended, and all that!'

'That's all right,' she smiled. 'It was my fault, if anybody's. Have you seen Geoff?'

'Doesn't the fact that I'm still in one piece answer that? Sorry! I haven't.'

Mrs Marshall was one of the first to be astir, and Helen repeated her question.

'My dear! Didn't he tell you? He was waiting up for me last night to say he was catching the plane back to the east coast today. Miles lent him the estate car and Ali to drive him to the airport. Naughty of him not to let you know.'

'That's all right,' Helen said, swallowing her disappointment. 'I was very tired last night, and if he told me it probably didn't go in. *I'll* be leaving on Tuesday, you know. Must get back to work.'

'I know, my dear. Now the wedding's over I'd like to get my house clear and settle down to normality myself. It has been lovely, though, seeing you again . . .'

CHAPTER TWENTY-FOUR

WHEN Helen presented herself at the Medical Services Administration block in the better quarter of Madras a week later, the only jarring note in the symphony of her life—now that she was returning to work—was Edward.

He had a cold, offended look about him as though he could nowadays scarcely tolerate her even as a colleague.

'You've had a good leave, I suppose?' he accused, for such was his tone.

'Yes, thank you, Edward,' she told him. 'I hope you're keeping well and—and happy?'

'Happy?' he scowled. 'Why shouldn't I be happy? I've never been happier, if you must know.'

'Good. I'm glad to hear that,' she smiled. 'Is my passage arranged, by the way?'

'I suppose it is. I'm a degree above that department, you know. Personnel Movement will give you all the gen. Was there anything else?'

Helen rose with dignity, deciding there was no earthly reason why she should ever see this spoilt man-child again.

'I must have come to the wrong office, Edward. I'm sorry for troubling you. Goodbye!'

'There was one thing,' he said hastily, not heeding her outstretched hand. 'A fellow was asking for you a few days ago.'

Helen's heart leapt.

'Was there any message?'

'My dear girl, I don't know. He may have left a note . . .'

'I see. Where would I find it?'

'Ask further down, old thing, would you? I have a conference and I'm late already.'

Helen spent a searing ten minutes seeking news of Geoff, for she was certain the caller had been he.

'I'm sorry, Dr French,' said the Indian clerk who dealt with Fan-Cho district. 'Anything which may have been addressed to you will have gone out in the mail, the usual way. Unless you ask for specific documents to be restrained, that's the procedure.'

'Of course.' Helen swallowed her disappointment. 'My passage is booked on the *Bim-Bom-Bay* sailing tomorrow at ten a.m.? Thank you, Mr Khalub. Thank you very much.'

She could scarcely sleep in her hotel that night for the noise of the storm which swept the coast, and her own speculative thoughts. Why had Geoff called to ask for news of her? Had he anything more important to say than had been said already?

At the docks she gained some enlightening information. Ships sailed when they could, these days, and another freighter, the *Fan-Y-An*, had sailed for Fan-Cho forty-eight hours ago with a European passenger on board.

'Geoff!' Helen breathed in thankfulness. 'He'll be there to greet me when I arrive.'

The thought sustained her throughout two and a half days of tossing passage through the angry seas. They were held up a further six hours off Fan-Cho, waiting for the tide to carry them through the gap in the reef. This journey was made in darkness for the first time in Helen's remembrance, and she scrambled out of the launch into her native friends' ready, welcoming arms and splashed her way through the surf on to the firm sand of the beach.

'Min Hana cum back!' the glad news went around.

'Hello and goodbye, Dr French!' said the waiting locum heartily. 'This has been the longest twenty-six days of my life. How you keep on sticking it, I can't imagine.'

'You're going on the *Bim-Bom-Bay*, Dr Seawell? She's a dreadful old tub. Even I was sick.'

'Can't feel her timbers under my feet quickly enough after the isolation here. I've left a report. Your manservant arrived two days ago. Queer character, isn't he? Come on, Abhar!'

The doctor and his bearer waded through the surf and climbed into the waiting launch, for the freighter was by now hooting impatiently out in the deeps.

Helen acknowledged Bahadur's salaaming figure absently, and pointed to her personal luggage which had been stacked on the beach by the welcoming islanders.

'Thank you all very much,' she called ringingly, 'and I'll see you in the morning. I'm very tired. I'm going to sleep now.'

They wandered off in chattering groups and she turned for one last desperate look about her, acknowledging the fear which had wormed its way into her heart.

'Geoff!' she called quietly.

If he was there he would hear her, sense all the desperation and longing in her tone.

But there was no response. Geoff simply wasn't there to meet her. He must have known she was coming—all the islanders knew—but he had kept away.

Now her fever lent her wings which carried her up to the house far ahead of Bahadur. Geoff's letter—she would read that and know what he wanted to say to her.

Maybe he was doubtful of her reception of his declaration of love and was keeping his distance until he knew how she intended to respond.

'That's it!' she decided, and was relieved to find the lamp lit in the living-room of the house, once she had forced her way in through the barricaded front door. Her mail was in two neat stacks on the desk, and she hurled most of this hither and thither as she sought a missive addressed in Geoff's firm, sloping hand.

She looked more carefully the second time, and still hesitated to acknowledge the gnawing fear within her as Bahadur staggered indoors with the luggage.

'Did you have a good leave, Bahadur?' she asked out of politeness and duty.

'Very good,' his hands fluttered amiably. 'My wife will have another child, I think, if she is not too old. My son at University he is a grand fellow now, but politics'—he shrugged—'all politics. Children learn politics now-days instead of how to earn a living. When they're all politicians there'll be fun, won't there? No rice in the paddyfields and nobody knowing how to get ore out of the mines . . .'

Helen cut him short in desperation.

'We'll talk about that tomorrow, Bahadur. Tell me, have you seen McLeod sahib?'

'Seen McLeod sahib?' the fingers twinkled. 'No, Memsahib. I have been far too busy cleaning the house after that untidy old doctor sahib and his worthless servant. A Madrassi man, that Abhar! A low caste fellow.'

'Didn't McLeod sahib come out on the same ship as you?'

'No, Memsahib. There was one white sahib on the *Fan-Y-An*. A very important sahib. He was charting new islands and reefs for the Government.'

'What about Ling John and Miss Huong?'

Bahadur looked blank and somewhat offended.

'Am *I* their keeper?' his liquid eyes enquired.

'It's all right, Bahadur,' she said tiredly. 'You can go to bed.'

When he had left the house she glanced again through her mail, noting one envelope addressed in flowery characters and without a stamp. This she opened without real interest. A single sheet of highly scented paper was withdrawn, then Helen stared as she saw the signature at the bottom was written in both English and Chinese. The message was brief and to the point.

'Dear Dr French,

'If there is anything to forgive between you and me, I ask that you be magnanimous and forgive.

'I would have you realise that our eyes, different in shape as nature made them, can never be expected to see things the same way. I never intended to take anything from you, only that you should not take anything from me.

'I'm glad the serpent did not bite you, or I could never be happy.'

Helen crushed the missive in her hand, feeling strangely numb inside.

Blossom Huong, it seemed, was seeking peace with her, or at least a cessation of the cold war between them.

Because the letter was both undated and unstamped it must have been delivered by hand. If Blossom was on the island she could perhaps, make real amends by confiding what had happened to Geoff.

Spurred on by this new hope, Helen put a coat round her shoulders, for the air was surprisingly cool, and plunged on up the now familiar path to Geoff's bungalow. She remembered the first time she had gone to see him, the blaring music, the surprised bather wrapped in a scanty towel, his amazement that such an apparently young innocent could be the island doctor, and the kiss which had warned. 'Keep away, if you don't want trouble.'

Searing memories they were, because they had indulged so much in defensive tactics it was quite clear, now, they were well aware of the nature of the possible offensive between them, and what it would involve.

'I never actually couldn't stick Edward until after I'd met Geoff,' Helen pondered in amazement, 'and maybe after Geoff had got to know me he knew what he must tell Celeste. And yet we wouldn't admit it. We were fools!'

She knew before she reached it that the bungalow was empty. There is a sixth sense we all possess which informs us when others of our kind are present, even though unseen.

Flashing her torch, she climbed to the front door, however, and straightened a tattered notice which was flapping in the wind.

PROPERTY OF GIDS, she read.

KEEP OUT.

She presumed GIDS meant Government of India Dental Services, as she herself belonged to the GIMS.

She knew what KEEP OUT meant, but, disregarding this, she pulled back the bolts on the door (bolts were always on the outside in Fan-Cho) and entered the antiseptically smelling building.

From room to room she went, and there, in the bedroom, was an old, torn bush jacket of Geoff's. But, apart from this small item, the bungalow was cleaned right out. Geoff had told her he would return to Fan-Cho for at least two months, but there was no indication that any of its recent occupants intended to come back here.

Helen realised that she must accept one of two facts: either that Geoff had lied to her, deceived her and run out on her, his brief passion having been born and declared only out of pique for her apparent neglect of him for another, or somewhere between Yan Udow and here they had managed—aided by misunderstandings and lost mail—to lose one another. If she clung to the second, as one clings to hope, there was nothing she could do here on Fan-Cho except prepare a letter for Geoff and send it c/o the GIDS on the next ship.

Wherever Geoff was on the mainland, he was the freer of the two to act, if he really loved her.

'*If he really loves me!*' Helen echoed her thoughts. 'I'm doubting him already.'

She picked up the torn bush shirt and caught the man-fragrance of him as she pressed it to her cheek.

'Oh, Geoff!' she cried out, her eyes stinging as though they wept tears of blood. 'Why are you hurting me like this? Why?'

CHAPTER TWENTY-FIVE

THE hurt was too deep for tears after a while and became a dimmed light in a pair of sombre grey eyes. Helen lost weight, slight as she already was, and her cheeks were sunken and remained sallow after she had battled her way through a bout of malaria without taking to her bed.

There was an outbreak of chills among the islanders after a tramp had called bringing a bosun who was suffering from 'flu. Helen had her hands full, and was glad of it. Even Vikrit was laid up and she had to tackle the clerical side of things as well.

Week had followed week, and now hope was shut away from her world in some sort of mental Pandora's box. There was no use in repining her lot; men had proved anathema to her peaceful doctor's existence. She must lose herself in work, allow her heart to calcify so that she could maintain a peak of efficiency which was impossible when one's desires were divided.

Thus, one day as she sat at her desk, she signed her name to a neatly typewritten document which ran to eighteen pages. It was her thesis on 'Albinism, its Causes and Effect', and was intended to earn her a fuller degree in the medical field so that she could demand a choice of jobs when she eventually returned to the United Kingdom to work.

She felt relieved to have got the thesis off her chest, and yet she knew there would be a blank in her life which must quickly be filled. At the least sign of a vacuum Geoff had a habit of rushing into her thoughts, and life was only bearable when she was keeping thoughts of Geoff at bay with other pursuits.

'Well, there it is!' she sighed as the typescript was sealed into a large envelope and addressed to London. 'What is it, Bahadur?'

The bearer announced the village carpenter, and this gentleman Helen welcomed, for otherwise she might have had straying thoughts.

'Yes, Kai-lam, what is it?'

'Min Hana,' the man bowed and then sat down on the floor, 'I am much troubled. My respected mother and father, we have a quarrel today, and now I hear they have gone back to their house on Ay-oh. This is very bad.'

Helen looked her most understanding.

'I'm sorry, Kai-lam. All families have quarrels. You mustn't blame yourself. They'll come back when they've thought it over.'

The man was not comforted.

'Min Hana, perhaps they do not come back. What then?'

'You must go and bring them,' she advised. 'Until the monsoon is over we must all stay together.'

'I know, Min Hana, but our catamarans are all washed out to sea in the last storm. My parents took our only boat. It takes time to make a boat which is seaworthy. The wood must be seasoned. You know that.'

'Yes, I know that, Kai-lam. I wouldn't worry for a day or two. I'm sure the old ones will return of their own free will if we leave them alone. If not I will go and fetch them in my boat. Does that make you feel better?'

The man suddenly struck his brow.

'Min Hana, I do *not* feel better. Tonight is the night of the Great Wave . . .'

'The tidal wave?' Helen asked, not prepared to argue,

for these people were invariably right about such things. 'Ay-oh is pretty high in the centre, and your parents will be sure to climb to high ground.'

'No, they will not,' the headman almost wept. 'That is what we quarrelled about. My father is an old man and foolish at times. He says the Great Wave is not due until next year, but he is wrong. This is the seventh year. Every seventh year a mountain of water washes through the sea and drowns these islands, all but the peak of Fan-Cho. Tonight you and your servant, all of us, must climb to the mountain and tie ourselves together with ropes. It is the only way we can continue to live, Min Hana.'

She looked a little dubious at last.

'Kai-lam, aren't you making this out to be much worse than it is? I've been here more than three years, and although the tidal waves during the monsoon are a little frightening, they're not as enormous as you say.'

'This is a seventh year, Min Hana, and you have not seen what you will see this night. I have lived many sevens of years, and it is as I say.'

'Then you want me to take my boat and get your parents, is that it?'

'If you will, Min Hana. If you will.'

'I will, of course,' she smiled, then looked blank suddenly. 'My man, Vikrit, is sick,' she said. 'Who else can drive the boat?'

'Simbat-lal, Min Hana.'

'Send him quickly. I don't like the look of the weather one bit.'

'Is there anything in all this seventh year business?' she asked herself as the tiny launch shot through the purpling sea. 'There's certainly one heck of a storm building up.'

The sky to the east was almost black, with neon signs

of wrath written against it. Not a breath of air stirred and
the sea was an uneasy, oily swell.

'Look! Min Hana,' Simbat-lal cried from the cockpit
of the launch. 'A ship!'

A great grey tramp was riding uneasily to the north-
west. She was further out than usual, and her launch was
putting in to the main island of the group.

'Mail,' Helen said without real interest, 'and probably
more shop for you.'

'Is good,' decided Simbat with a broad grin. 'Some
day I have real store with sun-blind.'

They beached on Ay-oh without much trouble, and
Helen went in search of the offended, sulking parents of
Kai-lam.

'Not come,' they both stated, over and over again.
'Not come. No good, Min Hana.'

She argued and argued, at last getting a bit annoyed
with the old couple.

'Then I must stay here with you,' she finally
announced, sitting down on a bamboo stool. '*I* can't
leave if you don't, and if the Great Wave does come
tonight I'll be drowned along with you.'

The old couple now exchanged troubled glances.

'The Great Wave comes next year,' the man wavered.

'Good; then we'll be all right, won't we?'

It was half an hour before the husband and wife
capitulated, and then Helen could scarcely get them
down to the beach quickly enough. The black curtain of
sky was creeping irrevocably nearer, though in the
actual vicinity all was still calm.

Simbat was now looking troubled as he delved into the
motor on the boat.

'Dirty plugs, Min Hana,' he announced. 'She won't
go.'

'Oh, goodness!' Helen looked at her watch. 'It'll be

dark in an hour, and sooner if the storm breaks. Do try to get the engine going, Simbat.'

Half an hour later came a phut-phut from the cockpit which did not peter out into a cough.

'Good!' Helen decided. 'Now let's go.'

Once they were clear of the island she saw the tramp making off in a northerly direction.

'Isn't she off course?' she asked.

Simbat smiled. 'Getting out of the way of the Great Wave, Min Hana. This is the time when ships which are not careful are never seen again.' He cocked his thumb downwards. 'The fish know better than some people. They have gone too.'

'Put the light on,' Helen said as they approached the reef, for now almost the whole sky was blacked out. 'You've piloted very well, Simbat, but watch out now, for goodness' sake!'

The searchlight failed to come on, however.

'Just a minute!' Helen said as she groped in her medical bag and the boat nosed towards the gap in the reef. 'I've got a torch here.'

Simbat started the engine again and Helen hung over the prow of the launch flashing the torch around her.

'Inch in,' she called. 'Slowly does it.'

She was never more amazed in her life when her torch revealed a swimmer in the water.

'Geoff!' she mouthed soundlessly.

'This way,' he called clearly. 'Follow me and then let me get aboard.'

As he climbed over the side Helen gently put her oilskin about his gleaming shoulders. She couldn't speak. It was as though there was no need for words. The waiting was over, and that was all that was important.

The storm broke as the launch was dragged ashore.

'Leave it,' Geoff yelled above the screaming of the elements, 'and get inland. Climb for your lives!'

Geoff took charge of the old woman and Simbat the old man. Helen staggered along in the rear, happy enough in Geoff's regular, encouraging backward glances.

'Good!' he said as they began to climb. 'I don't know what's about to happen, but it's going to be hell let loose, and we're right in the middle of it.'

Trees were being felled like ninepins behind them, and then when the rain broke it was like a waterfall. One couldn't see or breathe for it and yet one was expected to climb.

Helen lost her footing. She went down and down, dazing herself.

'No turning back, my girl,' Geoff picked her up to tell her sternly. 'One way only. Up!'

'What about the old woman?'

'Her son had come down to take her. Are you afraid, if this is the end for us, Helen?'

'Not with you, Geoff. So long as we're together.'

'That's all I wanted to know.'

He picked her up and climbed with her, only pausing to kiss her protestations away.

'The end of the world or the beginning, Helen . . . who knows? This is the way I want it to be—with you in my arms.'

A cliff face lay ahead of them. Somehow they had missed the track.

There were voices from up above: many excited voices.

'Are you there?' called Simbat-lal.

'Here!' Geoff shouted.

'Wait for a rope. I am at the top of the cliff.'

Now there were lights, burning brands hissing as the

rain tried to quench them, and then there came one constant light, a torch and a new voice.

'Memsahib, where are you? Memsahib Doctor?'

Helen swallowed and looked up, startled.

'Bahadur's speaking! Geoff—he's found his voice!'

'Memsahib!' the voice was more anxious now.

'Maybe he doesn't realise he's speaking,' said Geoff. 'Don't shock him. Answer.'

'I'm here, Bahadur!' Helen shouted her loudest.

'Rope, Memsahib. Two rope. Pull when you ready.'

Geoff tied her to him, then wrapped the second rope around his thigh.

'Pull away!' he called.

They were bumping against the cliffside when they heard the dull roar of the tidal wave approaching. It grew to such a thunder that it was difficult to separate it from the more heavenly manifestations. When it struck Fan-Cho there was such an impact that the very mountain core shivered and shook as though about to disintegrate.

Helen was conscious of a rope which held Geoff against her in a comforting communion, then Bahadur's face peered anxiously into hers as he hauled her on to the plateau where the islanders were gathered together, Klantok the holy man in their midst, standing gazing at the lightning as though defying it to destroy him.

'Memsahib, you're safe?'

'I'm safe, Bahadur. Thank you.'

For a blessed while she knew no more.

The sun sailed benignly through the heavens as though nothing was amiss.

'What if two of your islands have disappeared?' he seemed to smile. 'You've got a lovely new one, which is very much better.'

'I still don't think I believe it,' said Helen, as she strolled with Geoff away from her flattened bungalow. 'Thank goodness the clinic stood up to things. That means we still have our drugs and supplies.'

'Now that your mind's at rest on that score can we talk about us?'

'We'd better,' she smiled mock-grimly. 'You have some explaining to do. You say you got my letter?'

'Yes,' he frowned, 'I did. A miserable apology of a thing which hoped I was well, etcetera. What do you mean by it, young lady? Why didn't you answer mine, as I asked?'

'I've had no letter from you, Geoff.'

'You haven't?' he looked aghast. 'First of all when I reported to my wallahs they told me I was needed in Eemoy, where scurvy had broken out, and that I needn't return to Fan-Cho as my researches were pretty complete and had told them exactly what they wanted to know. This meant letting Blossom know to wind up and get out as soon as possible as I needed her. I called at your admin. block and tried to see Courtenay, but he sent his secretary out to sheer me off, so I then asked how I could contact you. "Send a letter," they advised. "The mail always gets through." I asked if you'd be calling in person and they weren't sure. Anyway, I wrote you, *and* Blossom, and put the letter to you inside hers, asking her to deliver it. You really mean you didn't get it?'

Helen hesitated, seeing all now so clearly. 'Maybe it's somewhere in the wreckage of the house, Geoff,' she said quickly. 'It may have been overlooked.'

He held her by the shoulders.

'But you didn't read it?'

'No.'

'And what were you thinking?'

She buried her head against his shoulder.

'That life was pretty awful,' she admitted.

He kissed her long and lingeringly, sighing when their lips unlocked.

'Listen, sweetheart. That letter was asking you to give me a little encouragement during the waiting time, if you felt you could. I've had a pretty bad time too, but I couldn't accept as final something as insubstantial as mere silence. If you don't want me for a husband you've got to tell me so in the flesh. Tell me now. Say, "Geoff, buzz off and pull teeth," or something like that. I can take it.'

'Geoff,' she said solemnly, 'buzz off and pull teeth if you have to, but love me too. Love "till death us do part".'

He looked at her in silence for a moment, then a cry almost strangled him as he drew her to him.

'Send for Old Brother,' he shouted between wild kisses. 'Tell him there's to be a wedding here and we'll need him!'

'Geoff, we can't!' she laughed hysterically. 'We can't be married island fashion. Not us.'

'There's a ship coming in any moment now,' he announced, shading his eyes, 'and there'll be a captain on board who can do the necessary. Game?'

'I'm game,' she told him, dimpling, feeling a glory of love surging through her.

'And then do you mind spending your wedding night on Fan-Cho, like Va-tu did?'

'Of course I don't mind. I'd rather it was here than anywhere. I know this place, love these people, and they'll wish us well to the last man of them.'

She surrendered once more to the demand of his arms and lips, then he released her and pointed to the gap in the reef where a launch was nosing through.

'Here it is. Are you ready?'

'I'm ready, Geoff,' she assured him with fearless eyes, and gazed across the sun-dappled water which lay golden before her, indicative of the future.

Doctor Nurse Romances

Romance in modern medical life

Read more about the lives and loves of doctors and nurses in the fascinatingly different backgrounds of contemporary medicine. These are the three Doctor Nurse romances to look out for next month.

CRUISE NURSE
Clare Lavenham

CAPTIVE HEART
Hazel Fisher

A PROFESSIONAL SECRET
Kate Norway

Buy them from your usual paperback stockist, or write to: Mills & Boon Reader Service, P.O. Box 236, Thornton Rd, Croydon, Surrey CR9 3RU, England. Readers in South Africa-write to: Mills & Boon Reader Service of Southern Africa, Private Bag X3010, Randburg, 2125.

Mills & Boon
the rose of romance

How to join in a whole new world of romance

It's very easy to subscribe to the Mills & Boon Reader Service. As a regular reader, you can enjoy a whole range of special benefits. Bargain offers. Big cash savings. Your own free Reader Service newsletter, packed with knitting patterns, recipes, competitions, and exclusive book offers.

We send you the very latest titles each month, postage and packing free – no hidden extra charges. There's absolutely no commitment – you receive books for only as long as you want.

We'll send you details. Simply send the coupon – or drop us a line for details about the Mills & Boon Reader Service Subscription Scheme.
Post to: Mills & Boon Reader Service, P.O. Box 236, Thornton Road, Croydon, Surrey CR9 3RU, England.
*Please note: READERS IN SOUTH AFRICA please write to: Mills & Boon Reader Service of Southern Africa, Private Bag X3010, Randburg 2125, S. Africa.

Please send me details of the Mills & Boon Subscription Scheme.

NAME (Mrs/Miss) _____ EP3

ADDRESS _____

_____

COUNTY/COUNTRY _____ POST/ZIP CODE _____

BLOCK LETTERS, PLEASE

Mills & Boon
the rose of romance